H.A.

All through the city a ⟨...⟩
behind the present an⟨...⟩
There are threshold zo⟨nes,⟩ ⟨...⟩
where the laws of time and space falter. Strange
things can happen, the barriers between the worlds
grow thin and it is possible, just possible, to move
from one world to another . . .

Prepare to enter **H.A.U.N.T.S** – a strange terrifying world with forces of good and evil. Evil so deadly
that even the *ghosts* fear for their lives . . .

The H.A.U.N.T.S *Series*

1. H is for Haunting
2. A is for Apparition
3. U is for Unbeliever
4. N is for Nightmare
5. T is for Terror
6. S is for Shudder

H·A·U·N·T·S

T is for TERROR

CELIA REES

Hodder
Children's
Books

A division of Hodder Headline plc

Contents

1

Ghost-Hunters

'Hey, Davey, look at this.'

Davey's sister Kate held up the local paper for him to see.

Relics Return to Cathedral
'little short of miraculous'

Relics recently discovered in the old part of the city, and thought to be those of St Wulfric, founder of the Cathedral of St John the Baptist, are to be returned to their former resting-place after a period of more than four hundred years.

Provost Michael Campion told our reporter that the find was 'little short of the miraculous' and that there are plans afoot to restore the original shrine situated in the chapel that still bears the saint's name.

Davey Williams scanned the article. He had been there when the saint's relics had been rediscovered. He and Kate, along with their cousins, Tom and

Elinor, had played a vital part in getting them restored to their rightful place. He smiled to himself as he read. Although he knew all about this, it was still satisfying to see it in print. He was just about to give the paper back to his sister when his attention was caught by an article on the opposite page.

Ghostly Goings-on

Reports of ghostly goings-on have been pouring in from all over the city: everything from mystery monks moving past the cathedral in ghostly procession, to horsemen haunting Hollow Lane.

Hi-tech Chaos

Even modern offices are not immune. Firms situated off Market Square have reported hi-tech chaos: unaccountable computer malfunctions, mystery faxes and phantom photocopies.

Shiver Corner

At one of the city's oldest pubs, the Dyer's Arms on Harrow Lane, landlady Mrs Brenda Meakin tells of strange noises coming up from the cellar.

'Some nights it sounds like all hell's broken loose,' she says. Many a morning, Norman the landlord finds barrels moved, crates overturned, coolers and pumps turned off. Alsatian guard dog, Prince, normally known for his fierceness, refuses to go down there at all!

Other residents of Harrow Lane have reported a phantom horseman and eerie hoof beats at the dead of night. Running footsteps have also been heard along nearby Johnswell Passage. Such experiences are forcing residents to consider renaming the area 'Shiver Corner'.

Apparitions

The local tourist board might have seen this as an extra draw in a city famous for its ghost tours, but their offices on Butcher Row have also been hit: brochures and leaflets misplaced, computer files erased. Ghosts have been glimpsed here at regular intervals, dating back to the time when the building was an inn, *The Seven Dials*. Mrs Diane Jarvis, manageress of the Rosebud Café next door, also reports disturbances: cutlery hurled, glass and crockery broken.

Ghost-hunters Called In

Things have got so bad that local people have called in a team of ghost-hunters. Mrs Sylvia Craggs, psychic, medium and Chairperson of SIPPAP, The Society for the Investigation of Psychic, Paranormal and Associated Phenomena prefers the term 'paranormal investigators'. She goes on to say: 'The current outbreak may be linked to recent redevelopment in and around the old part of the city. We are taking it very seriously and I can confirm that we have been called upon to look into it.'

Davey studied the article carefully before handing the paper over to Kate. As she read down the page, her expression stayed serious and thoughtful. The reporter's jokey tone left her cold. She knew, as Davey did, that there was another city, a ghost city, existing parallel to their own. Something very serious must be going on there for it to show itself like this. She looked across at her brother. The inn of *The Seven Dials* was home to a ghost crew she and Davey knew well. Polly, Elizabeth and Govan lived there with their captain, the high-wayman, Jack Cade. Kate read the part about ghost-hunters again. She did not like the sound of that. It could mean trouble for their ghost friends.

'Maybe we could go in to town early,' Davey suggested. 'Check it out. I've got a feeling . . .'

Kate nodded. There was no need for him to say more. There had been a time when she had dismissed Davey's 'feelings', his intuitions and premonitions, as fantasy, laughed at them even. Not now. They had been through too much for that.

'If we went in straight away,' Davey went on, 'we could have a scout round before we have to meet Tom and Ellie. What do you think?'

Tom and Elinor, their twin cousins, were coming to stay for a combination of the Mayday weekend and Kate's birthday. Their bus was not due in until 6:30, which left plenty of time . . .

Davey stood up. 'Let's go, then. Have a nose about. Find out what's happening.'

Kate and Davey took the bus. They had to get out at the terminus in the new part of the city. Open tour buses were the only ones allowed into the Old Town.

They crossed the river and made their way up Fore Street to the cathedral and the Market Square. As they passed the Market Cross, Davey kept an eye out for the board advertising Haunts Ghost Tours. Davey always looked out for it. It reminded him of the tour they had gone on last midsummer; their first visit to the hidden city. He jogged Kate's arm. The

Haunts Tours board wasn't there any more. Neither were any of the others. All the ghost tour notices had been removed.

To Davey this seemed ominous, but Kate thought that there was probably some simple explanation.

'Let's ask her,' she pointed to a familiar figure: Louise, their Haunts Tours guide from last midsummer. 'She ought to know.'

Louise was lounging next to a City Walks hoarding and no longer sported flowing black gothic clothes. Her ample form was squeezed into a skirt and blazer and, instead of carrying a staff with a plastic skull on the top of it, she wore a straw boater as her badge of office.

'Hi,' Kate said. 'You used to do Haunts Tours, didn't you? We went on one last year. It was really good. We wanted to go again, now the nights are getting lighter, but there's no sign out. What's happened?'

'Haunts has gone out of business,' Louise replied. 'Temporarily, so they say, but I don't know so much. Tell you one thing,' she gave a slight shudder, 'I won't be working for them again.'

'Oh, why's that?'

'Got a bit too *real* for me,' the older girl shivered again, despite the warmth of the day. 'Especially in the underground city. You remember down there?'

Kate nodded. The heart of the Haunts Tour was a visit to sad remnants of streets and dwellings, now built over and forgotten. They lay under the present city levels. Kate remembered them well. Even now, she could recall the damp stone smell.

'Well, it was always kind of atmospheric,' Louise looked nostalgic. 'I didn't mind it then. It was a good laugh, winding up the punters, but it began to get really creepy. All sorts of people began seeing things and hearing things – you didn't have to be psychic – and then things started happening.'

'What kinds of things?'

'All kinds. Sudden changes in temperature, objects appearing and disappearing, lights going on and off for no reason. Rocks falling. The door jamming. Freaked me out that did – I thought we were locked in. Management said it was damp getting in, all that building work making it unstable. Whatever the reason, it was downright dangerous. And some of the noises . . .' she hugged her arms to her, violet blue eyes wide with remembered terror. '. . . enough to chill the blood.'

'What kind of noises?'

'Screaming, shouting, crying, sounded like a barrel-load of banshees. Management said it was "amplified traffic noise".' Louise snorted her contempt. 'They have *got* to be joking! It was so bad in the end that I handed in my notice.' She pushed back her boater. 'Thought I'd try my hand at straight tours instead.' She peered over their shoulders at a group of advancing tourists. 'And I think I've got customers, so you'll have to excuse me. Like I said,' she added, as she got out her book of tickets. 'I wouldn't ever work for Haunts again.'

2

The Banishing

Kate and Davey went across the square and on into the oldest part of the city, threading their way through the picturesque warren of streets, following the signs to the Tourist Information Office. They were following roughly the same route as they had taken last year on the Haunts Ghost Tour. Davey stopped every now and again to test the atmosphere. He remembered getting goosebumps just about here last midsummer. He'd had this feeling that someone was following them; he'd kept thinking he heard a soft footfall and light whispered laughter. He turned again, knowing now that it had been Elizabeth, but this time he felt nothing.

His psychic sense had developed a lot since then. More importantly, he had learned to trust it, to believe in his premonitions, his sudden insights and powerful intuitions. He had learnt not to deny that he had them and not to fight them. He knew how to open himself up and let the feelings flow through him. He did that now but again felt nothing. No indication of any kind of presence, of Elizabeth

or anybody else. After what he'd read in the news-
papers, after what Louise had just said, he had
thought to pick up a world in tumult. Maybe his
psychic sense had deserted him?

On the other hand, maybe the ghosts had left this
part of the city. Been forced out by the ghost-
hunter's. He looked around, but his eyes were
unseeing, and into his mind came an image of a
city torn by war. One area full of frantic activity,
while another lay deserted and empty. He was
suddenly sure that the same thing was happening
here. They were in a battle zone, walking through a
war they could not see, and at the centre of it stood
The Seven Dials.

Davey stood for a moment in front of the large
black-and-white building on Butcher's Row where
the inn had once been. It was now the Tourist
Information Office. He looked up, his head cocked
to one side, hoping to hear the ghost of a laugh, see
the flicker of a face in the diamond panes. But there
was nothing. He glanced towards the café next door,
the one that had been mentioned in the newspaper
report. He had haunted that with Elizabeth. Davey
thought of her now; visualised the two of them
together. If she was around, then surely thinking
about that would bring her out? But the air was
neutral around him. He felt nothing.

Davey followed Kate into the Tourist Information Office. The large room was a centre of activity. It was a Saturday at the end of April so there were plenty of tourists there, leafing through the brochures, asking about accommodation. Kate and Davey paused by the door. Davey looked round and then gave a slight shake of the head; still negative. A little red light winked from a small white metal box fixed in a corner between the wall and the ceiling. Davey wondered fleetingly what its function might be, then turned away with a shrug. It was probably some kind of miniature closed circuit video camera, or 'electronic eye' security system.

Kate showed the newspaper article to the woman behind the desk and asked if she knew anything about it. Kate said she was doing a project, always a favourite way of getting adult co-operation. Not this time, though. The woman didn't seem to want to talk. She said they were too busy, to come back another day.

'What shall we do now?' Kate asked as they got outside.

Davey looked round the courtyard. It was not exactly like it was when the place was *The Seven Dials*. The main features were the same: the cobbled floor, the gallery running round, the half-timbering. But the age-silvered wood and pale brown plaster

11

had been given a smart coat of black and white. Tables from the wholefood café in the corner spilled over half the cobbles. Small shop units had been set up round the sides. People were milling everywhere. There was no possibility of making any contact. The site had about as much atmosphere as a supermarket.

'Hello, you two,' a voice said behind him. 'What are you doing here?'

Davey turned to see Dr Jones, the young archaeologist from the City Museum, smiling down over a brown paper sack of shopping. For a moment he wondered what she was doing here herself, then he remembered that she lived in a flat above the Tourist Information Office.

'We're, er . . .'

'Doing a project,' Kate put in, nodding towards the Tourist Board door.

'Together? I thought you went to different schools?'

'We do. It's Davey's project. I'm giving him a hand.'

Mari Jones shifted the bag to her other arm. 'What's it about? Maybe I can help.'

'I don't think so,' Kate said quickly.

'Yes,' Davey said at the same time.

'Well, make up your minds,' Mari Jones flicked her dark red hair back and looked down at them, her greeny-brown eyes laughing and quizzical. She shifted the weight of her bag again. 'Tell you what? Why don't you come upstairs with me? I can dump this lot and then we can have a cup of tea and you can tell me all about it.'

Dr Jones's flat was one big room. Thick beams ran through uneven whitewashed walls and exposed rafters spanned the wide oak-planked floors. The sparse furnishings had been carefully chosen to allow the beauty of the old building to show through.

'Did you see in the paper?' Mari Jones came from the kitchen area carrying a tray of tea. 'The relics are back in the cathedral.'

Davey nodded. He and Kate had been there at the Easter rescue dig when the bones of the saint had been found. After that, they had been involved in a struggle to save them from those, both living and dead, who had been bent on stealing them for their own evil purposes. Dr Jones had played her own part in keeping the relics safe from harm.

'How did you convince the cathedral authorities that the bones belonged to St Wulfric?' Kate asked.

'Ultimately we can't be absolutely certain that they do belong to him, although the carbon dating puts them mid-seventh century, which fits with the historical record. This is the really interesting thing,

13

the clincher if you like.' She leaned forward to pour the tea. 'You remember Dr Monckton?'

The two children nodded. They took their cups from her silently. The sinister archivist had been in league with the most evil presences in the ghost city. The forces he had almost succeeded in unleashing had been absolutely terrifying. How could they forget?

'Well,' the archaeologist sipped her tea and continued, 'you know those papers he was working on?' They nodded again. The papers had come from the Judge's house. 'Among them was an inventory from the Benedictine Priory. Those monastic houses were huge, like small cities, with highly organised bureaucracies. Periodically they would list all their assets: the things they owned. Relics were highly valued, and among the barrels of this and sacks of that was a description of the relics, right down to the piece missing out of the skull. Now the bones might or might not be those of St Wulfric,' she spread her hands, 'for all we know he might not even have existed, but they *are* the relics that the monks reverenced; the inventory proves it. So there you have it. Now,' she sat back, arms folded, 'what are you doing here?'

'We – we,' Kate started.

She was unsure what to say, but Davey looked up

and met the archaeologist's sharp gaze. He hesitated for a moment and then reached into his pocket and fished out the page from the newspaper.

'We came because we saw this,' he said as he handed over the crumpled paper.

Mari Jones smoothed the creases out on her knee and began to scan the article on 'Ghostly Goings-on'.

'I see,' she said, when she had finished reading. She folded the paper carefully before returning it to Davey.

'We just wondered . . . Well, what we wondered was . . . Oh, thanks . . .'

Davey took the paper from her and then made a fuss of re-folding it and putting it in his pocket. He could not think what to say.

'You live here,' Kate put in. 'Maybe you could tell us what's been happening. I mean, why were the ghost-hunters brought in?'

Mari Jones didn't answer straight away. She looked at the two of them sitting side by side on the sofa. They were very different. One fair, one dark; one tall and willowy, the other short and thick-set; but they both had the same intense look on their faces, the same level of interest in their eyes. There was something strange about them, she'd felt it before – especially the boy, Davey.

'Well,' she leaned forward, 'it's pretty much as you

read there. There was a certain amount of disturbance downstairs, probably a glitch in the electrical systems, but someone mentioned poltergeists. Then the cleaners start seeing things, sensing presences. One of them is psychic, apparently, and she pronounced the spirits who live here to be "deeply unhappy". Next thing you know, they've brought in these people. I think it's some kind of publicity stunt, personally. Get people into this place and boost interest in the city . . .'

'What people?' Davey asked. 'Who are they exactly?'

'There were two of them, a man and a woman.'

'What did they do?'

'Some kind of exorcism, I should imagine. I wasn't there, so I'm not sure. The woman called it "a Banishing", the man said it was "a Cleansing".'

'How do you know, if you weren't there?' Kate asked.

'Because they offered to do the same thing up here. Perform the same ceremony or whatever. Odd couple. She seemed all right, a bit cold and standoffish – more I don't know, old-fashioned, like a medium or something. Talked about 'interceding with the spirits'. He was different. All high-tech. Brought in a shed-load of equipment. Even left a little gizmo down there to keep it clear. I wasn't sure about him.' She shook her head. 'I reckon he was a bit of a con artist. Anyway, I didn't want him messing about up here.' She looked round the beautiful tranquil room with the afternoon sun slanting through diamond panes. 'This is an old building. I chose to live here because of it. If it has ghosts, I'd consider that a plus.' She shrugged. 'They are welcome to stay.'

'So you believe in them?' Davey looked at her. 'Ghosts, I mean.'

'I wouldn't go quite that far,' she laughed. 'But in my line of work we come across some strange things.' She leaned forward, suddenly serious. 'Oh, you won't find them written up in journals and papers, but occasionally things happen that can't be explained in any ordinary way.' She stood up and went over to a bureau, opened the top drawer and took something out. 'Take these, for example. You know the Johnswell, where I met you once – I told you we did a dig there?' They both nodded. 'Well, during the dig, I found these.' She held out the objects for them to see. A football medal and a fifty pence piece. Davey and Kate did not look at each other. 'Nothing strange about that, you might say, except they were found with objects from the seventeenth century. Even then,' she began to pace up and down, the objects clasped in her hand, 'such finds could be put down to modern contamination of the site, thrown in by a passer-by, fallen out of someone's pocket. Except, except,' she held them tighter now, 'this particular fifty pence piece was not in circulation at the time it was found, and this particular player was not even in the league, let alone the England team. Strange, eh?'

Davey and Kate nodded and looked away. They had seen the objects before. They had thrown them into the Johnswell themselves.

'It's an anomaly,' Mari Jones added, as she continued to pace the room. 'There is no rational explanation. I come across examples all the time. Like I said, you won't find it reported in academic papers, but some of my colleagues find dowsing, someone holding a couple of sticks, far more reliable for locating sites than geophysics. There are other things, too.' She stopped her pacing and stood still in the centre of the room. 'Sometimes, when I've been out on site somewhere remote, up on the downs, say, or the high moorland, and it's late in the evening, or early on a misty morning, and there's no one else around, then I've felt it. I've never actually *seen* anything, but it's hard not to feel the presence of all the people who've lived, and worked, and worshipped, and died there. Perhaps over thousands of years.' She gave a slight shiver. 'I don't know if that's what people mean by ghosts, but if it is, then, yes,' she turned to them with a smile, 'I guess I do believe, and I don't think that anybody should interfere with them.'

'Like those people, you mean? The couple who came to see you?'

'Yes, Davey, like them.'

'I still don't really understand what they actually do,' Kate said.

'Hang on a minute.' Mari Jones went back to the bureau from which she had taken the finds and came back with a card. 'Here. They gave me this.'

She handed the card to Kate. It read:

Society for the Investigation of Psychic, Paranormal and Associated Phenomena
Chairperson: Mrs Sylvia Craggs
Psychic Consultant: Eugene Hutton FIPR
13 Fiddler's Court
Old Town

'If you want to know more about what they do,' Mari Jones said, 'I suggest you go and see them.'

3

The Society

Before they went to the Society's offices in Fiddler's Court, Davey suggested a quick detour. He wanted to go to Keeper's Stairs, to see if there was still a way into the underground city. If there was, he explained to Kate, then they could go to the Room of Ceremonies and use the mirror to get through to see what was really happening.

Kate was not keen on this idea at all, but she knew how hard it was to deflect Davey once he was set on something. If she did not go with him, he was likely to go on his own, and Kate hated to imagine the consequences of that. It was safer for her to go along with him and pray that they could not get in.

Kate's prayers were answered. Not only was the door locked, but it was secured with a hefty padlock. Davey rattled this a couple of times and turned away disappointed. He was desperate now to know how things were within the ghost city. The disquiet he had felt before had been growing all the time that Dr Jones had been talking. It was turning now into a fever of frustration.

'Never mind, Davey.' Kate flicked the card Dr Jones had given to her. 'Let's go and find out what this lot are up to.'

The Society for the Investigation of Psychic, Paranormal and Associated Phenomena – SIPPAP for short – and formerly known as just the Society – had occupied the same premises in Fiddler's Court for over a century. The Society had been set up in 1887 by a Doctor Aston, a medical doctor who considered himself to be both a scientist and a philosopher. His stated aim was to 'examine in a scientific spirit those phenomena, both real and supposed, which defy rational explanation'. He had quickly attracted other like-minded persons to him and the Society had grown to become one of the country's foremost organisations dedicated to the investigation of matters related to the after-life, mediumship and the paranormal. They had investigated everything from full-scale hauntings to table-rapping, and had an almost unrivalled collection of case histories. The Society had declined in recent years, both in membership and reputation, to become a rather old-fashioned, sleepy organisation, its work largely ignored and forgotten, carried on by a few stalwarts like Mrs Sylvia Craggs.

Not any more. Recently the Society had experi-

21

enced a transformation, both in membership and fortune. It now had its own magazine and website. Under the guidance of Mr Eugene Hutton, Psychic Consultant, SIPPAP investigated a host of unexplained phenomena, from UFOs to crop circles, the perfect organisation for the twenty-first century.

Kate and Davey knew none of this as they stood in front of the tall grey stone town house set back from the street behind freshly painted black iron railings. Wide stone steps led up to a large front door with a polished brass knocker in the shape of a lion's head. Kate and Davey mounted the steps and stood, undecided about what to do next. The knocker was seldom used, the hinge was stiff with the white residue of brass polish. Kate looked round for some kind of bell or buzzer and saw a row of them set into the wall. She pushed the button next to the initials: SIPPAP. The Society no longer took up the whole building. The offices were on the upper two floors.

A squawk from a small loudspeaker made Kate jump.

She pressed another button, and stood on tiptoe, speaking into the little grille.

'Hello? Is that the Society?' She waited a second and then carried on. 'We'd like to come up and talk to you. We want to know more about what you do.'

There was no voice reply, but a buzzer sounded

and the lock clicked back. Davey reached down and turned the brass handle.

They pushed the door back, leaving it slightly ajar, and walked in to a wide hall with grey polished stone-flagged floors. Heavy cream-painted doors led off right and left, but these were firmly shut. Davey and Kate walked on towards a mahogany banistered staircase twisting away to the upper storeys. Davey was suddenly reminded of Derry House. He'd gone in there at Hallowe'en and the place had terrified him. His footsteps faltered and he half wanted to run, but he made himself go on. This was not the same at all, he told himself. Kate was with him, for one thing, and they were here in broad daylight. This was not some dark, dusty, deserted, paper-peeling, rat-infested, crumbling dump. This building was used all the time. There was a vase of fresh flowers and a pile of mail stacked on the table under the stairs. All the doors had little brass plaques showing the names of the companies. The hall smelt nice and fresh, of scent from the flowers and lavender floor polish, not all dank and damp.

'I put them there myself.' A voice from just above their heads made them start. 'Lilies. My favourites. Such a divine smell. Some don't like it, of course. Reminds them of funerals.'

Kate and Davey looked up to see a woman leaning

23

over the curving banister. She was tall and thin and stern-looking, with strong features and a prominent high-bridged hawk-like nose. She was middle-aged, even older, but wore her hair long, swept back from her forehead. Her black hair showed no grey, apart from one streak of white at the front on the right-hand side. Her eyes were darker than Davey's, almost black; they watched him now from under hooded lids.

'I never forget a face,' Mrs Craggs said and smiled, showing prominent ivory-coloured teeth.

Davey knew her, too. She had been in the Rosebud Café when Elizabeth had shown him how to haunt. Elizabeth had warned him to be careful of her. The woman was a medium and she had seen them . . .

Davey began to back away, but he was a fraction too late. The big front door shut with a loud click as a long arm shot out and strong fingers gripped him firmly by the wrist.

4

Mrs Craggs

'Just checking for a pulse,' the woman said and then released him. 'You'd better come up,' she added, jerking her head towards the floor above.

She turned with a swirl of her floral skirt and Kate and Davey followed her up the stairs to the Society's offices.

'Like I said, I never forget a face,' her hooded black eyes brooded on Davey. 'Now who are you? And what do you want? And don't lie to me,' she shook her ringed forefinger at him. 'I'll know in an instant.'

'I – I'm,' Davey cleared his throat and started again. 'My name is Davey Williams and this is my sister Kate.'

'Sylvia Craggs,' the woman introduced herself. 'Sit down, sit down.' She waved towards two hardback chairs covered in boxes. 'Shift that rubbish. That's right. Now what can I do for you?' She asked again when they were seated.

'We've come to see you because we read about this—' Davey took out the newspaper story and spread it out. 'We know, about the ghosts, you see, particularly the ones at *The Seven* Dials, the Tourist Information Office as it is now. We want to know what's going on, if – if they're safe, and—'

'Wait! Wait!' She held up her hand and moved to a large untidy desk. 'Get rid of these for me, there's a good lad.' She picked up a heap of papers and handed them to Davey. 'Box by your feet. That'll do. Now, how did you get into this?' Sitting down, she picked up a pencil, pushed a small portable typewriter out of the way, and reached for a yellow legal note-pad. 'I think you'd better start at the beginning, don't you?'

Davey did as he was told. He thought back and told her about all the things that had happened to them since last midsummer. Starting from when they first went through the portal in the underground city, to the battle for the relics in the basement of the museum. Kate listened while he spoke, occasionally adding a detail or two to back him up, but he seemed to be getting on fine. Her attention soon wandered to the room itself.

The room was strange, intriguing. She had not expected to see computers and fax machines for one thing. She looked above the level of office clutter to the portraits of past presidents that lined the oak-panelled walls. Dark paintings of austere Victorians ranging up to modern photographs of men in lounge suits: doctors, scientists, churchmen and psychics, ghost-watchers all, looked down with penetrating eyes. In between them, the walls were hung with photographs of the most haunted places in Britain: gaunt ruins etched against open skies; hulking castles brooding at the end of tree-lined avenues; gloomy rectories with steeply pitched gables and tall chimneys, half-hidden by leafless branches, blank windows hiding secrets. There were churches, inns, sprawling manor houses and squat suburban villas, all neatly named and framed, caught in stark black-and-white.

There were other photographs too, still more chilling and mysterious. Kate thought at first that they were just blurry, out of focus. Then she realised. The mist round the fat woman's head was ectoplasm: A milky white substance, pouring from her nose and mouth. The fuzzy effect in the centre of another photo was not due to camera shake, it was a picture of a ghost caught halfway up a flight of stairs.

Davey was nearing the end of his story now. Kate found it difficult to tear her fascinated attention away from the walls and back to her brother. She looked from him to Mrs Craggs to see what effect his words were having on her. The woman was absorbing this tangled tale of ghosts and entities without a single flicker of doubt. Occasionally, she made Davey stop, or repeat something, while she made notes on her yellow pad in loopy flowing writing, but then she waved him to go on again. We've come to the right place, Kate thought. Only here would such a strange tale be believed.

'We heard that you were getting rid of them. The ghosts, I mean. "Cleansing" is the term we heard,' Davey said as he finished. 'We came to see if that was true.'

Sylvia Craggs did not reply immediately. She looked down at her notes, checking through the things that this boy had told her, assessing his story. She saw no reason to disbelieve him. As a medium, she was quick to recognise psychic power in others. Rarely in her life had she come across such ability, especially in one so young. To have been to the other side and come back again . . . This was quite exceptional.

'Tell me, Davey,' she said after a while. 'Do you know the term "chime child"?'

'Yes,' Davey avoided her searching gaze. 'Yes, I do.'

Kate looked up. She'd never heard it before. 'What's that?'

'A child born on a Friday, within the chime hours,' Mrs Craggs explained. 'Some say as the clock strikes twelve, others between midnight and cockcrow.'

'What's so special about that?' Kate asked, suddenly nervous. She knew that term applied to her brother. She knew the time of Davey's birth.

'Chime children are gifted. They can see ghosts and fairies . . .' That accounts for a lot, Kate thought. 'They also have immunity from ill-wishing,' Mrs Craggs went on.

'They cannot be "looked over", watched from afar. They love and control animals, they have a way with herbs and healing . . .'

'I thought they were also unlucky—' Davey mumbled.

'Who told you that?' Mrs Craggs' black eyes were sharp upon him.

'Just – someone – someone who knows a lot about folklore.'

Miss Malkin had told him that just before Christmas. Davey shivered as he thought of her. She was The Lady. The Old Grey Man's daughter. She was not a ghost. She was something else altogether. She was a member of the Host, the Unseelie Court. What did Jack Cade call them? Eldritch – fey, faerie. Davey had been careful to leave all mention of her out of his account.

'I have not heard that,' Mrs Craggs said after a moment or two. 'But I do know that chime children are good at keeping secrets.' She gave him a knowing

29

look and her mouth twisted in a half-smile. 'Now, back to the matter in hand,' she looked down at her pad. '"Cleansing" is not a term I would use. I prefer "Banishing",' she said, staring down at her pad. 'Do not mistake me, I'm no friend to ghosts and spirits. They don't belong in the world of the living. They should move on, travel forward to the place where they belong. But I believe in persuasion. I would not want to force any suffering soul trapped here in spirit. Unfortunately, not everyone in the Society shares this view.' She looked up. 'My colleague, the chap you see pictured there, is keen to use other, more aggressive, methods.'

She nodded towards the newest portrait on the wall, a big colour photograph of a man who appeared to be of indeterminate age, neither old nor young. Formally posed, in a black suit, white shirt and black tie, he looked more like a businessman than a medium. His short dark hair was brushed back from his forehead, his small moustache neatly clipped. Pale eyes stared out from behind gold-rimmed glasses, making him look cold, rather distant. He seemed ordinary, almost nondescript, next to the other more flamboyant portraits.

'Eugene Hutton,' Mrs Craggs waved her hand in his direction. 'Our next President. Very forward-thinking. He has plans for us. He's demonstrating his new method this very evening in front of a *very* carefully selected audience. He wants to take us into the twenty-first century. But I'm too old for this sort of thing,' she indicated the computers and fax machines. 'The Internet and glossy magazines. Look what he's done to our journal!' She brandished the latest copy of *Ghost-hunter*, with its lurid cover. 'It used to be called *Afterword*. I'm leaving. Hence the cardboard boxes.'

'Does that mean you won't help us?' Davey slumped in disappointment.

'I didn't say that, did I?' She regarded him with her dark hooded eyes. 'I am a medium. I *could* open a channel to the other side.'

'Would you do that?'

Davey sat forward, waiting for her answer, relief and excitement rising inside him, but the silence stretched on as the woman stared straight ahead. She seemed to be looking at something over his shoulder, and then Davey felt it, a prickling presence as if someone was standing behind him.

'There is someone who wishes to contact you . . .' Mrs Craggs's normally deep voice became even deeper and her heavy eyelids began to droop. 'A young girl, about Kate's age, dressed in Victorian clothes. She is very agitated. What she has to say is very important . . .'

She stopped speaking abruptly and her breathing took on a heavier, almost snoring quality. Suddenly, she pitched forward until her head was nearly on the desk. Davey turned to Kate in alarm, fearing that the woman might have been taken ill, but his sister motioned him to sit back. Mrs Craggs was going into a trance.

She snapped back, sitting upright in the chair now. Her black eyes were open, but they stared forward, seeing nothing. When she spoke again, her voice was utterly different. The tone was light and silvery, her words quick, rapid with impatience. She was speaking with Elizabeth's voice.

'Davey! Kate! Oh, I'm so glad! I thought that I'd never get through to you. I thought that woman would never stop blathering! Using a human medium is so *very* tedious!'

'Are you all right?'

'Yes, for now, but there is war in the city, Davey. The Judge is taking his revenge for what happened in the museum. His Sentinels are giving no quarter. He has issued a Declaration, anyone listed is annihilated. But it is not just Sentinels we fear.' Her voice dropped to a whisper. 'There are these others. We call them the Invisibles. They can strike anywhere, at any time, without warning. They are clearing the city of ghosts; soon there will be none left. None!'

She broke off, trying to calm herself. 'You have to help us, Davey. You have to make them stop.'

'What happens when the Invisibles come? What happens to you?'

'We disappear.'

'How? Where to?'

'We don't know. No one ever comes back. But it is not what should happen.' Her voice dropped to a whisper. 'It's murder.'

'What about the others? Govan and the Blind Fiddler, Jack and Polly?'

'We were scattered after the clearance of *The Seven Dials*. The Blind Fiddler is less vulnerable than we are. He is not a ghost in the strictest sense. But as to his whereabouts? No one knows. Perhaps he is with the Host. I am with Jack. He is leading the resistance, but things are not going well . . .'

'What about Govan and Polly?'

'There are rumours,' Elizabeth's voice became shaky, indistinct. She paused for a moment. 'Rumours that they have been taken.'

'Taken? Where?'

'The Judge's house. Some are taken and kept there for reasons that we don't understand. Everything is very confused, Davey. You have no idea. We are harried and hunted, caught between the Judge's Sentinels and the Invisibles. We think they are ghost-hunters from your world, in league with the Judge and the Prior, like Dr Monckton.' Her voice faded to nothing and when it came back it was low and husky, without any of its usual buoyancy. 'If help does not come soon, we are doomed.'

Before Davey could ask anything else, Mrs Craggs' head fell forward on to her chest. She lapsed into deep regular breathing as if she were now asleep.

'What should we do?' Davey whispered to Kate.

'I don't know,' his sister shrugged. 'Wait for her to wake, I suppose.'

Davey leant forward to shake her.

'No,' Kate held his arm. 'It's best to let her come round naturally.'

'How do you know?'

'I read it somewhere. Now keep quiet.'

Davey found waiting and keeping quiet difficult. He could feel the strength of Elizabeth's distress, sense her fear. There had to be a way to help her. He owed his life to her. She had saved him from The Lady.

Mrs Craggs was coming out of her trance now. 'Anything useful?' She asked, fixing the children with her fierce black gaze.

'Don't you remember?' Kate said.

The medium shook her head. 'Never remember a thing. Some mediums do, Eugene for instance, but they have someone on the other side who acts as a spirit guide. I do not. When I'm speaking in spirit, I'm but a conduit. Does a radio remember the words spoken through it? So you'll have to tell me what the girl had to say.'

Sylvia Craggs listened carefully to Kate's account and then sat back in her chair, eyes closed, fingers steepled.

'This Judge's house. Does she mean Judge Andrews?'

'Yes,' Kate replied. 'How do you know?'

'It's the most haunted house in the city.' Mrs Craggs stood up and went to the window and looked over the square. 'Number 1, Fiddler's Court. It even has its own website.' She turned back to face them. 'It's very well-known in ghost-hunting circles. That's why Eugene chose it for this evening's demonstration.'

She handed them each an invitation. Selected guests were invited by Mr Eugene Hutton to see for themselves the effectiveness of his ghost-hunting apparatus and to witness its extraordinary powers.

'How does his system operate?' Davey asked in a quiet voice.

'Not my department, I am afraid,' Mrs Craggs shrugged. 'Haven't got a clue.'

'But it does work?'

'Oh, it works all right. I've seen it with my own eyes.'

'How? How does it work?'

'Some kind of ray we'd have called it in my day, energy force, I suppose. Anyway, this ray, or whatever it is, makes the spirits materialise, and then another one sucks them away again like some kind of psychic Hoover.'

5

Eugene Hutton

'Where is he now? This Mr Eugene Hutton?' Kate asked

'He was in the building earlier, but I think he might have gone to test his machine.' She reached for a fax. 'We had a request for help from Prima Electronics. Their headquarters are near here. He was thinking of using it for a dry run.'

Davey was not really listening. He was still staring at the address on the invitation. 'This demonstration – we've got to stop him!'

Mrs Craggs shook her head. 'You won't stop him. You don't understand. Eugene is staking his reputation on tonight's performance. There will be all kinds of people here, reporters and journalists, as well as other paranormal investigators. He will not call it off.'

'Why do you want to stop it, Davey?' Kate looked at her own invitation. 'Why is it so important?'

'Don't you see? These 'Invisibles' Elizabeth talks about. It's this Eugene Hutton and his ghost-buster machine, it's got to be!'

37

'Eugene doesn't like the term "ghost-buster",' Mrs Craggs remarked absently.

'What if it is?' Kate frowned. 'If he's using it to get rid of the Judge and the Sentinels, wouldn't that be a good thing?'

'But he's not, is he?' Davey shook his head violently. Kate could be so stupid sometimes. Why couldn't she see? Davey took a deep breath and turned back to his sister. 'Polly and Govan have been collected – to be guinea pigs. Kept with the rest of them, like rats in a lab waiting for Eugene to zap them. We must find a way to warn Elizabeth and the others.' He turned to Mrs Craggs. 'Can you get in touch with her again?'

'I can try,' Mrs Craggs closed her eyes. 'But I'm not a telephone line, you know.' After a moment or two she shook her head. 'No one there, I'm afraid.'

'Oh.' Davey was bitterly disappointed. The only other way was for him to get into the ghost city. But how? The route he had taken before, the mirror in the Room of Ceremonies that acted as a portal, was no longer accessible; the door to it was padlocked. He shut his eyes tight, trying to concentrate. There had to be a way to help them, there had to be; but the more he tried to think of one, the more tangled his mind became and the more hopeless it seemed.

38

Mrs Craggs watched him closely. She had rarely seen such raw psychic power, but the boy was untrained. He had not learnt to channel his ability. His mind was a prey to strong forces, dragging him this way, that way.—

'That's not how you do it,' she said suddenly. 'You must clear your head. Relax. Empty your thoughts. Dismiss them one by one.'

Her words calmed him, cutting through his confusion. Davey did as she said and gradually felt the tension leaving his body. The surge and beat of each separate thought receded, like surf withdrawing from a beach. At first there was nothing. Then the ghost of an idea came stealing in, and with it, as if born on the wind, the distant sound of a violin.

'Come on, Davey,' Kate was shaking his arm.

'What? What is it?' He felt strange, confused, as if he had been sleeping.

'It's nearly time to meet Tom and Ellie. We have to go.'

Eugene Hutton looked down from the small round window on the top floor of No. 13 Fiddler's Court. Adjusting his gold-rimmed glasses, he watched the two children leave by the front door. He could have gone downstairs to enquire of Mrs Craggs who her visitors were, but he didn't have to. He knew.

Anyway, they had been having such an interesting conversation, he would not have dreamt of interrupting. There was nothing paranormal about how he'd heard them, just everyday eavesdropping. An oddity of design in the ancient central heating system meant various sorts of hot air got piped round the building. Most convenient. He did not plan to change the central heating system in his general update.

A tiny smile pursed his small mouth and developed into a little wheezing chuckle as he thought of all the changes he planned to make. He would have no trouble ousting Mrs Craggs. After tonight's little demonstration they would probably make him President for life. He cracked his spidery fingers. His system had taken years to perfect. He had tested it to destruction on every major ghost haunt all over the city. He nudged the large aluminium box by his feet. It was scientifically brilliant and absolutely foolproof.

He'd explained it all to Mrs Craggs, but she was too old and stuck in her ways to understand. She thought it was cruel. He had dismissed her objections as trivial. Ghosts were ghosts, they didn't feel anything. She had completely missed the point.

Tonight's demonstration was all set to make him

40

and his organisation world-famous. He intended to record what happened with special camcorders and cameras, capturing ghosts on film and video for the first time ever. No fakes. No special effects. This would be real. The resulting footage would be worth millions . . .

Behind his gold-rimmed glasses, his icy grey eyes glazed even further as he gazed into a future filled with fame, wealth and success . . . He glanced down at Davey's round dark head as the boy left the square with his sister. The child was smart. Clever. He had guessed correctly at Eugene's intention, but as for stopping this evening's experimentation? Just let him try.

If Davey had been a little less preoccupied, he might have sensed the man spying on him. If he had looked up then, the boy's sharp eyes might have been able to discern a dark form standing by the man's side, hovering by his shoulder, as close as a familiar. Mr Hutton's spirit guide. A medieval monk, known as Prior Robert . . .

Davey did not sense any of these things. He was concentrating his whole mind on trying to read the signs that would point a way into the ghost city . . .

He stopped in the middle of the Market Square and looked around.

'What are you doing, Davey?' Kate pulled his arm. 'We can't stop here. We're late already.'

'I need to find the Blind Fiddler.' Davey replied, refusing to move.

'Can't it wait until we've been to the bus station?'

Davey shook his head. 'There's no time for that. I need to do it now.'

Kate closed her eyes and sighed, mentally counting to ten. Sometimes her brother's behaviour tested the very limits of her patience. She tried to talk to him, reason with him, but he wasn't budging. She looked at him, assessing his stubborn, shut-off expression and felt herself crumble, being forced to give in. She was more practical, more acquainted with the wider picture. Her mind moved along more than one track. She looked at her watch. Tom and Ellie's bus was due in any minute. If there was no one there to meet them, the complications could be awesome.

'Okay, okay.' Kate looked down at her brother. 'You stay here. But wait, Davey. Do not disappear. Do not go wandering off. Are you listening to me?'

'There's just one little thing I want to check out, that's all,' Davey replied. 'It won't take more than a couple of minutes. Then I'll come straight back. I'll be here, I promise.'

Above them the cathedral clock chimed the half-hour.

'You'd better be.' Kate shouted over her shoulder as she went sprinting off.

6

The Portal

Davey headed for the great doors of the cathedral as soon as Kate left Market Square. He had not lied to her. Finding the Blind Fiddler, or not finding him, would take only a couple of minutes. What happened after Davey found him, however, could take a while longer . . .

Davey was following his hunch that he would find the Blind Fiddler in or around the cathedral. He wasn't outside, playing his violin, busking in the Market Square, so he had to be inside somewhere. Davey made his way over to the small side chapel that had once contained the shrine of St Wulfric. This was where the Fiddler had been waiting the last time, but now the whole chapel was temporarily screened off.

Davey risked a look behind the plastic sheeting.

'Hello, there.' A boy of about eighteen or nineteen looked up from where he was working. 'Can I help you?'

'Oh, er, I was just wondering why this bit was closed off.'

The boy stood up and removed his protective goggles. White powdery dust smeared across his dark face. He held a chisel and mallet. His callused hands were covered in little scars and nicks, and were so dusty he looked as though he was wearing white gloves.

'We're restoring the shrine of St Wulfric. It's okay, you can come in if you want to.'

'Thanks.' Davey stepped over the threshold. 'What are you doing now, exactly?'

'I'm helping to build the screen to go there, see?' He indicated the recess behind the altar that had housed the original shrine. 'It was smashed at the time of the Reformation. We're making another one. Me and the other trainees.'

Davey looked at the stone tracery the boy was working on. The stone was light, almost blue-white, against the time-darkened grey of the rest of the cathedral. The carving was sharp-edged with clean fine lines. The design of the grille was very simple, plain even, but the delicate carving made it beautiful.

'We're just putting on the finishing touches.' The boy held his arms wide. 'It's got to fit in flush, see?'

'It's fantastic.' Davey walked round the delicately carved screen. 'Brilliant. You're doing a great job.'

'Thanks.' The boy smiled in acceptance of Davey's appreciation. 'But it's not just down to me.'

He turned back to his work and Davey was just about to leave when the boy called out to him.

'Is your name Davey?'

'Yes.' Davey looked back in surprise.

'I just remembered something. There's an old bloke, he's blind, busks violin out in the square. Usually has a young lad with him, but he's been here on his own lately. Anyway, he said to keep a look-out for you.'

'Do you know where he is now?'

'Could be in the Old Garden. Through the door by the Lady Chapel.'

Davey thanked him and left. He found the door and let himself into a walled garden, planted with all kinds of herbs and sweet-smelling plants. Davey could smell sage, rosemary, lavender as he brushed past. The garden was quite a suntrap, it was warm and still and filled with the sound of bees. Davey looked around, thinking at first that there was no one in there, but then he saw the Blind Fiddler sitting on a wrought iron bench tucked away in a corner. He held out his hand as Davey approached.

'Davey! Welcome!' he indicated for the boy to sit next to him. 'I often come here.' His fine nostrils flared to inhale the scents around him. 'It is good to feed the other senses.' He pinched off a shoot from

the bush by his side. 'Verbena. Proof against fairies.'
He smiled at Davey and held the crushed leaves for
him to smell. 'Now,' he spread his thin, long-
fingered hands on his knees, 'why did you summon
me?'

Davey looked at him in astonishment.

'I didn't know I had.'

'Well, somebody did. Perhaps your powers are
greater than you think. What do you want of
me?'

Davey took a deep breath before answering. He
knew what he wanted to do was crazy. But something was telling him to trust his instinct.

'I need to go into the ghost city. Elizabeth needs
me. I want to help her and the others. I don't know
how, but I know I can.'

'Hmm.' The old man thought for a moment.
'Things are bad in the city, very bad. What you
propose could put you in dire peril.'

'I know that. But I'm prepared to take the risk. I
won't be a nuisance. There's a man involved, a bit
like Dr Monckton. I think I know what he's pro-
posing. Having me there, on their side; might even
up the chances . . .'

'Perhaps. But your presence might also prove a
hindrance. They will have to worry about you as
well as themselves. That is why I am here. In your

47

world. They have enough to do without caring for a blind old man.'

'All I want is for you to tell me how to get into the city. I can't use the mirror in the Room of Ceremonies. The door to the underground city is locked. Will you help me?'

The Fiddler did not reply straight away. His blind eyes roved over the sheltered garden, unable to see but taking in the old brick walls, mellow in the evening sunlight, the wide beds of shrubs and flowers laid out round a green lawn, close-clipped and perfect, as smooth as baize cloth.

'You could be putting yourself in considerable danger,' he warned again.

'That is why I want to go alone. Without Kate and the others,' Davey replied. 'Jack's crew have done it for me, risked themselves lots of times, particularly Elizabeth. I owe them a debt.' He searched his mind for a phrase Jack had used. 'A debt of blood.'

'Very well.' The old man leaned forward, his long fingers clasped round the top of his staff. 'Take this path.' He rapped the tip on the ground.

Davey looked down at the brick path beneath his feet.

'Follow it clockwise to the far corner of the garden. There in the wall you will find a door. It is the old Pilgrim's Gate, the way into the cathedral precincts taken by those on their way to the shrine of St Wulfric. Go through the door and you will find yourself where you want to be.'

Davey got up. 'Elizabeth and the others – How will I find them?'

'They will find you. Now go. While we are still here alone.'

Davey did as instructed, keeping his eyes on the uneven brick path, following it round to the opposite side of the garden. When he got to the corner, he looked up. At first he could see nothing. He even wondered if the Fiddler had been lying to him. The walls' face was half-covered in some kind of creeper, but behind that Davey could see that it was blank. Just a mass of small red bricks capped by a roof of coping stones. Then, as he stared on, the wall began to change . . .

Behind the tangle of creeper, a door began to appear, set into a thick stone archway. The arch at the top was round. The bottom disappeared into the ground. It was obviously from a time when the ground here was on a different level. The door itself was made of wood, thick oak slabs studded with metal. At the side was a handle made of twisted iron. Davey stood for a moment, hesitating, then he heard voices behind him. The whole door became

49

transparent and began to fade, shifting like a hologram. It was now or never. Davey took a deep breath. Stepping forward, he grasped the twisted circle with both hands and turned.

7

Ghost City

As Davey stepped through the gate, the world changed around him. He hesitated for a moment, wondering if he hadn't made a big mistake. He looked behind, but the door in the wall was disappearing. It was already too late to go back.

He gazed around, uncertain as to what to do, or where to go. He was in Knowlegate, the ancient roadway that led up from the river, along past the cathedral and into Market Square. A stream of people were surging along in front of him. Men, women, children. Some in family groups, some alone, some carrying bundles and household goods, others walking empty-handed, but they were all heading in the same direction, as if fleeing from something.

As the ghosts streamed past, he noticed that every age and time was represented; it was like watching some bizarre pageant. Normally the ghosts did not mingle. They were divided into crews and they stayed in their own haunting grounds. Something serious must be happening for them to become all mixed up like this. Davey slipped into the throng unnoticed. In his dark T-shirt, black jeans and black trainers, he blended in easily enough. Anyway, the ghosts were too preoccupied with their own troubles to take much notice, that is if they saw him at all. Ghosts did not always see the living, Davey reminded himself; in this world he was the ghost.

He was wondering if any of them could see him, when a woman stopped in her tracks and stared at him, peering up into his face. Then she clutched her shawl closer and backed away.

'You have a look of my son,' she said by way of explanation. 'I search every crowd, every face, just in the hopes . . .' She bit her lip. 'Are you alone?' She looked at Davey again. 'Have you lost your family?' Her worried expression softened into pity. So many had. So many young ones had been separated, left to wander alone since the Cleansing had begun.

Davey shook his head. 'I have no family. I've lost my crew.'

'Come.' She linked arms with Davey. It was her duty to look after him, help him, as any mother would, in the hope that some other mother might be caring for her own son. In the face of the Judge's cruelty, it was all that they could do. 'Come with me,' she repeated. 'It's not safe out in the streets. *They* are coming . . .' She looked fearfully behind her, pale eyes wide, her gaunt face etched with terror. 'We must not be caught out in the open like this.'

'Who? Who's coming?' Davey asked as she dragged him into the ghost tide.

'The Sentinels! They are clearing this part of the city! We must go! We must flee! The curfew bell will soon be sounding. Anyone out after that,' she shuddered, 'can expect no mercy.'

'I'm looking for Jack Cade,' Davey said as they struggled through the crowd. 'Do you know him?'

'The highwayman? I know him by reputation. They say he is gathering ghosts to him in an effort to stem the destruction.'

'Do you know where he is?'

'No, no,' the woman shook her head. 'He keeps on the move constantly. They hunt for him in every part of the city. Clearing it, emptying it, section by section. So far he has evaded their searches. Some say he is to blame for this affliction that has come upon us, but I say all strength to him. He is our only hope.'

At the mention of Jack's name, a man turned towards Davey. He was small and dark, youngish-looking, with long hair straggling out from under a battered cap. His face was deeply scored and marked, his clothes ripped and torn as if he had been in an accident.

'You looking for Cade?' he asked.

Davey nodded.

'I know where he is,' the man smiled, revealing a line of uneven blackened teeth. 'I can take you to him, if you like . . .'

'No, no. It's all right, really,' the woman replied before Davey could say anything. She gripped Davey's arm tighter and hurried on.

'Wait up, Missis.' The small dark man put out a hand to restrain them. He signalled to others forming around him with a slight motion of the head. 'We've been told to look out for such a one.'

'Then you must be mistaken. This boy is my son.'

The woman pulled on Davey's arm, dragging him again into the thick of the crowd. Davey could hear voices raised behind them, a hue and cry starting. People were surging all around them, pushing and jostling like frightened animals. Up ahead, the way was narrowing. The general flight was about to turn into a stampede.

The woman looked up, sensing the panic spreading around them.

'We must go back. We are entering a trap.'

'How do you know?' Davey looked behind. The road was solid with people.

'The Sentinels. Don't you see them?'

Davey looked up. The way ahead was walled by shadows.

54

'They set up where the road narrows, forcing the crowd through in ones and twos. Then they can pick off whoever they choose. You have already been selected. That man you were speaking to? He is one of the Judge's own crew. The Recent Dead.'

Davey shuddered, remembering his narrow escape on his first visit to the ghost city. He did not want to be caught again.

'Down here, quickly.' A boy dodged out from the crowd and motioned them to follow him.

The woman hung back, holding Davey to her. The boy turned, beckoning frantically, as the crowd parted. In the distance, Davey picked up the purr of motor-bike engines. Motor-bikes were the Recent Dead's preferred mode of transport. Davey hesitated no longer. He moved to follow the boy.

'Don't go,' the woman shouted, gripping his arm tighter. 'It could be another trap—'

'I have to take my chances.' Davey gently removed her hand. 'Don't worry. I'll be all right.' He went to go, then turned back. 'Your son. What's his name?'

'William.'

'I'll look out for him. Tell him you're okay.'

'Good luck.'

'You, too.' Davey meant to say more, to thank her, but the woman had gone. The crowd was thinning now, melting away at the edges, dispersing in all directions. It was almost time for the curfew bell.

The boy led Davey into a maze of the narrow alleys that lay behind the main thoroughfare. After the noise and confusion behind, this area was eerily quiet. Davey followed the boy's echoing footsteps. Above his head a single bell began sounding monotonously. That must mean the curfew. Davey had no idea of what lay ahead of him, but nothing could be worse than waiting in line like cattle, trapped between the Recent Dead and the Sentinels with the curfew bell tolling above his head.

8

Invisibles

'Jack sent me to get you,' the boy said when Davey finally caught up with him. 'The Dead ain't the only ones directed to look out for you. Now follow me. We gotta move fast now. Keep close and silent. Ain't safe on the streets once the curfew sounds.'

The boy he was following was about his own age or younger, with a shock of red hair in sharp contrast to his dead-white face. He wore a grey shirt and black trousers shiny with dirt and grease.

'Up here!'

The boy led Davey down between rows of tenements. The buildings were tall, perhaps five or six storeys. They leaned over, almost meeting, allowing only the minimum of light to filter down to the narrow street. Davey had never seen this part of the city. The whole area had been declared structurally dangerous, not to mention insanitary, and had been pulled down many years before he was born.

'This one!' The boy dodged under the sagging eaves, dragging Davey in through a doorway with a splintered frame and rotting lintel.

They ran up and up a tightly turning staircase. The banisters were rickety, missing in places, forcing them to keep into the wall. The stairs themselves were treacherous: the bare boards worn and splintered, some of them loose and broken. The smell of mould and decay was almost over-whelming. The skirting boards were holed by rats and plaster was falling in rotting lumps from the walls.

'Here we are.' The boy whispered, rapping lightly on a door right at the top of the building. 'That's if they haven't had to move again.'

'Who's there?' a voice came back.

'Matty. Matty Groves. I've got a party with me, wants to see Jack urgently.'

'What party?' The door opened a crack.

'The lad called Davey. He's from the Living. He's the one—'

'Why didn't you say straight away?'

The door opened and the man there stepped respectfully out of the way.

'Come with me.' He scuttled off, beckoning Davey to follow him.

Jack's headquarters took up the top floor of the whole block. Rough holes had been knocked through from one tenement into another, providing different sections with different functions: rest area, command centre. The last area was a field hospital. This was where he found Elizabeth.

'Davey!' She jumped up from the patient she had been attending. 'I knew you'd come!'

'What is the matter with them?' Davey looked around at the wounded lying all about, pale and silent, stretched out on low roughly made-up pallets.

Elizabeth's pretty face changed. All the bright excitement at seeing him drained away.

'Some of them have been caught by Sentinels. Some by the Invisibles. We cannot treat what afflicts them.' She sighed. 'Other than keep them comfortable, there is little we can do.'

'I have news,' Davey said. 'That's why I came. It's about the Invisibles, as you call them. Is there still no sign of Polly?' He looked round for Jack's fiancée, hoping to see her working among the wounded.

'No,' Elizabeth shook her head. Her wide clear brow contracted and her grey eyes clouded with worry. 'Nor Govan. They have almost certainly been taken.'

'What happened?' Davey asked quietly, knowing how much they both meant to Elizabeth. The mute boy, Govan, she regarded as her brother and Polly had been like a mother to her.

'Polly went out after curfew, to help collect the wounded. Govan went with her. Neither of them came back. For a long time we knew nothing. Then word came that they are held as prisoners in the Judge's house. There can be very little doubt. He's trying not to show it, but Jack is beside himself.'

Jack was out on the roof right at the far end of the building. Elizabeth hitched her long skirt above her knees and led the way up the narrow spiral staircase. A door opened out on to a wide flat roof studded with shallow glass domes, put there to shed light into the stairwells below. Jack was leaning over a low parapet, looking through a thin brass telescope out into the darkness descending over the city. Above him the sky contained no stars, no moon, just a deep charcoal greyness deepening to black.

The highwayman turned at their approach and held out his hand in greeting.

'Davey! Welcome!' His dark face was serious, marked with lines of worry and tension, but when he saw Davey his stern expression relaxed into a smile. 'We are in great need of good friends. Tell me, what news do you have?'

'It's about the ones you call the Invisibles . . .'

Jack listened carefully as Davey told him everything he knew about the Society, what he suspected about Eugene Hutton and his special equipment.

'It is as we thought . . .' Jack sighed after Davey

had finished. He himself had suspected living ghost-hunters. Nothing else would explain this enemy they could not hear and could not see, prowling the city, striking at any time, at anybody, friend or enemy, as if all ghosts were its foes. 'But just one man, you say?' He shook his head and began walking up and down the narrow space next to the parapet. 'That is hard to believe . . . Where will he strike next, do you know?'

'That's what I came to tell you. He is giving a special demonstration . . .' Davey paused, his heart beating hollow at what he was about to say. 'It's to be held in the Judge's house. He's going to show this machine he has, he's going to use it . . .'

Jack Cade stopped his pacing and stood absolutely still. His dark eyes widened as he stared at Davey and his pale face tightened, flinching slightly as if he had just received a physical blow.

'But not on the Judge, or his evil crew, I'll be bound.'

'No,' Davey shook his head. 'I don't think so. I'm – I'm sorry, Jack . . .'

The highwayman turned from them, and stood for a moment looking out to the far horizon

'You bring grievous news. You must forgive me . . .' He leaned forward, arms spread, leaning over the parapet. 'This man and his machine – what he does is terrible Davey, quite terrible. There is a sound beyond all hearing, it is as if your ears are bleeding. Then, nothing. Anyone, everyone, in the vicinity disappears. Be they one or twenty. There is nothing left. Ghosts are destroyed where they stand. All, all . . .'

He began pacing the roof again, pounding his first into his hand. Elizabeth and Davey moved together instinctively, backing away from his dark raging fury.

Jack stopped his pacing and looked at them.

'All means Judge and Sentinels. They are ghosts, too . . .' He paused, arms folded, deep in thought. When he looked up, his eyes had lost their look of bleak despair. 'That is one thing we have noticed. Sentinels arc never in the vicinity when the Invisibles come to call.' He looked out over the parapet. 'After curfew, there is a lull in their activity, as if they make way . . . but what if it is not that at all? What if they dare not show their presence, because to do so would be dangerous . . .' A hint of a smile lightened his features. 'I begin to have an idea . . .'

Jack called for his lieutenants and was soon deep in huddled discussion.

While he waited, Davey leaned over the parapet, trying to work out where they were in the city as he knew it. He picked up the telescope near his hand and looked out over the surrounding rooftops. They fell away in steps down towards Fiddler's Court. He could make that out plainly, even see the front of the Judge's house. He pulled back as he saw Sentinels like long black shadows stealing into the square, returning from patrolling the city, moving in pairs, dark-robed and hooded, casting black beams left and right.

'The Sentinels are easy to spy on,' Elizabeth said as she stood by his side. 'They never think to look up. That's why we keep to the rooftops.'

Davey moved the telescope round, looking out for other landmarks. Up and to the right lay the cathedral, a dark indistinct bulk of stone in the grim grey gathering night. Down the hill to the left lay the sprawl of little streets that contained *The Seven Dials*. Below that ran Harrow Lane and Keeper's Stairs . . .

Which meant that they were standing approximately . . . The world blurred as he turned quickly to look over the rooftops on the other side. There could be no mistake. Up there was Fore Street, with the law courts and the City Museum. This must be the old Stanley Building, headquarters of Prima Electronics . . .

'Oh, no,' Davey groaned.

'What's the matter, Davey?' Elizabeth turned, thinking he was physically ill.

'We have to get out of here. Quickly.'

The sickness he felt was at his own stupidity. He had been so concerned about warning Jack about the planned demonstration at the Judge's house that he had completely forgotten what Mrs Craggs had said about Eugene Hutton going out for a trial run . . .

'What?' Elizabeth frowned.

'We've got to go now!' Davey looked round frantically. 'Tell Jack! Hutton will be here any minute! Everyone's got to get out!'

It was too late. From below them came a strange low surging boom, like some other sound enormously slowed down. It was almost below the level of hearing, an airborne vibration set at a frequency to break the world and everything in it. Davey felt himself gripped by it, his body, his face, his jaw, even his eyeballs were shaking. From below came screams and cries and then silence. Across the roof, one by one, the sky-lights lit up from below with a sickly chemical blue-green glow. The ghost-hunter had arrived.

9

Disappearance

'He said he'd be here . . .' Kate was standing with her cousins, Tom and Elinor, staring at the Market Cross.

'Well, he's not, is he?' Tom looked round, hitching the straps on his shoulders. His rucksack was getting heavy. There was absolutely no sign of Davey. They had looked everywhere, searched the Market Square. The cathedral was closed to the public, so he couldn't be in there. Tom turned back to Kate. He didn't want to seem unsympathetic, but she knew what Davey was like. She must have been crazy to leave her brother on his own in the first place, even for a second.

'He must have gone into the ghost city,' Elinor said. 'Found a way in.'

'How do you know?' Her brother looked down at her.

'I don't, not for sure, I've just got a feeling . . .'

'Don't you start,' Tom snorted. 'One psychic's enough.'

Elinor shook her head. 'It's not to do with being

psychic. It just stands to reason. If he isn't here, he must be somewhere else.'

'*Brilliant* deduction,' her brother shook his head in mock wonder. 'Thanks, Sherlock.'

'I think she's right.' Kate said, ignoring his sarcasm. 'As soon as my back was turned, he must have legged it . . . I knew he was up to something when he wouldn't budge . . .'

'Maybe he's gone back to that Society place you were telling us about,' Tom suggested. 'If he *has* gone into the ghost city, that Mrs Craggs person might be able to tune in to him. She is a medium, after all.'

'She's not exactly a short-wave radio, though,' Kate looked at her cousin. 'What if she can't?'

'Then we'll have to think of something else. Either way, we get to dump these.' He pulled at the straps of his pack. 'My backpack is killing me.'

It was just past seven o'clock, the traditional time for the curfew bell to sound, when Kate, Tom and Elinor presented themselves at the Society's offices in Fiddler's Court.

'What's the matter, child?' Mrs Craggs asked, as soon as she saw Kate's face. 'What's happened? Where's your brother?'

'I – we – don't know,' Kate looked round. Worry

was really beginning to gnaw away at her now. 'I thought he might have come back here.'

'Haven't seen him. Sorry. Any idea where else he could be?'

'Well, yes. That's the trouble,' Kate looked at Tom and Elinor. 'We think he might have found a way into the ghost world, the one we were telling you about.'

'Why would he do that?'

'When we left here, he was very concerned about what Elizabeth had told us.'

'Elizabeth is the spirit girl who spoke through me?'

'Yes, that's right. Davey wanted to go and help her and the others, but we had to meet Tom and Ellie. I mean, we couldn't just leave them at the bus station. We – Davey and me – had a bit of an argument. I left him in the Market Square. I made him promise he'd wait there, but when we got back . . .'

'He was gone?'

'Yes.'

'I see,' Mrs Craggs sat at her desk, her large hands clasped together. 'No-where else he could possibly be? Tried home?'

Kate shook her head. There was no way he'd go back there, not with all this going on, she thought. It would be hard to phone without giving away that something had happened. Mum'd go crazy if she thought that they had lost Davey.

'If he is in the spirit world,' Mrs Craggs paused to think. 'I might be able to get in touch . . .'

'That's what we were kind of hoping.' Kate glanced at her cousins again.

'Of course, I can't guarantee . . .' Mrs Craggs changed what she was going to say, in response to the distress on Kate's face. 'But I'll certainly try. Now. While everything's quiet. Before our guests arrive and before Eugene – Mr Hutton – comes back.' She looked at her watch. 'He won't be long. He's only gone to the Stanley Building, just across the back from us. Prima Electronics . . .'

'The computer software company?' Tom asked.

'Yes. Do you know it?'

'Of course,' Tom was surprised that anyone might think he didn't. 'They make games. What's he doing there?'

'Carrying out a trial run before tonight's demonstration. Computer companies have been particularly sensitive during this current wave of activity. We had an urgent request in,' she showed Tom the fax, 'only today. It's the ideal site for Eugene to test the equipment he intends to use tonight.'

'This equipment,' Tom asked. 'What is it exactly? How does it work? Do you know?'

'Haven't a clue. I told Kate and Davey earlier,' Mrs Craggs nodded towards Kate, 'I don't hold with gadgets. My powers lie in other areas.' She turned back to Kate. 'Let's try and contact your brother, shall we?'

Kate, Tom and Elinor sat quiet as Mrs Craggs went through the same routine as before. Once she reached her trance state, Kate leaned forward, on the edge of her seat, waiting for her to speak. But this time Mrs Craggs did not do the strange snoring breathing, or speak in different voices. Her dark hooded eyes blinked a couple of times and she sat back with a shake of her head.

'I can't get through to him or anybody else. I'm sorry, my dear,' she reached out and patted Kate's hand. 'Trouble and turmoil are creating static. We'll have to try later when things calm down.'

In the world of the dead, no one had time to deal with enquiries from the Living. Ghosts were pouring on to the roof, trying to escape the horror surging up from below. All those who could walk or crawl. The others were destroyed where they lay. Jack Cade was trying to organise an orderly evacuation: trying to quell the panic, dividing the jostling pack into lines across a roof where the skylights sparked and fizzed with bright spurts of light, as if a spot-welder was being used directly beneath them.

Ghosts filed towards the far edge of the roof. From there they were directed by Jack's lieutenants on to the next building and the next, across the city to safety.

Davey helped until there was no one else left.

'Your turn, Davey,' Jack urged him forward gently. 'Off you go.'

Davey looked to the next roof where Elizabeth was waiting for him, beckoning. The space between was not far, perhaps a metre and a half. Nevertheless, Davey hesitated. He was not normally scared of heights, but the chasm between this building and the next plummeted ten metres at least. It made him feel sick. Not just that, the dull booming thud coming up from below seemed to reach deep down inside to the very core of his being, stunning his senses, making him feel weak. Davey could feel his strength draining. He could hardly stand up, let alone leap. He couldn't even see properly. He blinked, staggering slightly. He would have fallen if Jack had not caught him. His arms and legs felt all floppy and he just wanted to lie down.

'Go, Davey,' Jack repeated. 'Go now for God's sake!'

He shook Davey by the shoulder, but the bones seemed to melt under his fingers, it was like gripping an empty sleeve. The highwayman looked down, his dark eyes full of concern, his pale face marked with fear and alarm. This boy was from the Living. He should, therefore, not be harmed by the Invisibles, but Jack knew the signs. The clouding of the eyes, the bluish-green tinge to the skin. It was what happened to ghosts just before they disappeared.

10

The Ghost Machine

All around Eugene Hutton the screens were going crazy. He had warned the company to shut down the system. If they lost files, that was their look-out. Hutton turned off his own instruments one by one and packed them carefully in to the different sections of the custom-built aluminium carrying-box. The test run had been satisfactory. More than satisfactory. There was no point in running down the batteries.

He had uncovered quite a nest here. Quite a rookery. The place had been swarming with presences. These were all unseen until he'd brought out his trusty machine, but now he had it all on camera. Eugene Hutton took considerable pride in the system he had perfected. It was of his own devising. A perfect combination of the old and the new. Prior Robert, his spirit guide, directed him to the area of activity; the machines did the rest. It could not be more simple. Eugene Hutton smiled to himself as he picked up the case. He had invented a genuine ghost-busting machine. He disliked the term but it was useful shorthand for what the apparatus did. The results were on film. It was going to make him a fortune. He looked around and saw typical high-tech office premises. There was no outward sign of the devastation and havoc his equipment had reeked, just a ghostly residue hanging in the air like ozone.

His good humour lasted until he got back to the Society and found those children were back with Mrs Craggs. Not only that, she had invited them to that evening's demonstration. He nodded acceptance of the fiction Mrs Craggs was giving him, that these were her nephew and nieces, but he regarded the three of them with suspicion. The older girl with the long fair hair and pretty blue eyes was the one he had seen from the window. But where was the little dark-haired boy? He had been replaced by two others. A lanky, sandy-haired lad and a girl who was clearly his twin. This was a mystery. Eugene frowned. He didn't like mysteries. At other times, he might have consulted his spirit guide, but Prior Robert was not available to comment. It was too dangerous for him to be near when the machinery was in operation.

Eugene stared down at them, unsure how to handle this. To countermand the invitation might invite suspicion.

'How does it all work, then?' the boy asked. 'Aunt Sylvia has been telling us all about the websites and everything. I'm *very* interested in your invention.' He nodded towards the aluminium box. 'I'd really like to know more about it—'

'I'm afraid that's impossible,' Eugene Hutton replied coldly. 'You'll have to wait for the demonstration, like everybody else.'

'Oh, surely not, Eugene,' Mrs Craggs intervened. 'Can't you give Tom a little sneak preview?'

'No,' he shook his head. 'That's impossible. Like I said.'

'That's a shame. Tom was looking forward to it.' Sylvia Craggs paused, regarding her colleague carefully. 'No one else has seen you use the machine except me. And I'm a bit of a duffer in the technical department. I thought Tom here could explain it to me. People are sure to ask what I think, they always do. Wouldn't want to say the wrong thing.' Her hooded black eyes narrowed on him. 'After all, psychic investigation has been plagued over the years by a great deal of trickery. Wouldn't want you accused of jiggery-pokery – would we now?'

Mrs Craggs let her words hang in the air, allowing Eugene Hutton time to take in her veiled threat. He stared back, his colourless eyes expressionless behind his gold-rimmed glasses as he weighed the possibilities. The old bat might be on the way out, but she still had clout. She could discredit him with the

Society before tonight's demonstration had even started. Against that, telling this kid here how it all worked seemed a small price to pay.

'There's not enough room in here,' he said at last.

'You can use your special room upstairs,' Mrs Craggs smiled.

'Come on, then.' Eugene Hutton picked up the aluminium box and jerked his head at Tom. 'Not that you'll understand.'

Tom grinned at his retreating back. 'Just try me.'

'Thank goodness he's gone,' Mrs Craggs slumped back in her chair with relief. 'Thought for a moment that he was going to dig his heels in.' She leaned forward again, elbows on the desk, fingers tented to her forehead. 'Spirits fairly clamouring, but they don't feel comfortable with Eugene in the room.'

'Is Davey there?' Kate asked.

'Wait a minute, I'll just see,' the woman swayed for a moment, eyes closed. 'He is there. But he can't speak just at the moment.'

'Why not?'

'He's had a shock—'

'What? What kind of shock?'

'That scoundrel you harbour, the Prior's cat's-paw, nearly caught him with his infernal machine . . .'

Elinor's mouth dropped open. She had not heard Mrs Craggs speak in trance before. Her eyes widened at the words, the sharp contemptuous tone. The voice coming from the medium's mouth belonged to Jack Cade.

'Is he all right?' Kate asked.

'He will be. He is resting. He has told us all about this Eugene Hutton and his evil machinery. I warn you, Mistress Kate, you must stop this man or we will all be destroyed. Do you know how he brings these terrible things about?'

'Not really,' Kate replied. 'Tom's trying to find out more about how it works right now.'

'Discover all you can. I have a plan . . .'

'What is it?'

'We are to give ourselves up to the Judge.'

'What?'

'I know, I know the risk we are taking, but truth be told, Kate, we have little choice. We cannot resist much longer. Our forces are much depleted, many are injured and wounded. We will be taken soon anyway and now Davey has told us what is intended for Polly and Govan and the others with them—' He broke off and Kate thought he had stopped, but then his voice came back again. 'We cannot take the Judge's house. It is too strongly defended. I had thought to break out from within, like the Greeks

76

and the horse they took to the Trojans, but, since speaking to Davey, I have another idea, but we must work together. Tell me, can you trust this human medium? For much depends upon it.'

'Mrs Craggs? Yes, I think so.'

'Good. Now this is what I propose . . .'

Kate and Elinor listened as Jack outlined his strategy.

'Now I must go,' he said at length, 'there is much to do.'

Kate wanted to ask more, not least about Davey's safety, but Jack's voice stopped as suddenly as it had started. Mrs Craggs was coming out of her trance.

'Well? What happened?' She demanded.

Her voice was as strong and brusque as ever, but Kate could see that the trance had taken it out of her. When she came round this time her face seemed more heavily lined, her eyes a little more sunken, her cheeks bleached of colour.

'Are you all right?' Kate asked.

'I'm fine,' she said, though her hand on the desk was trembling. 'But the experience can be rather draining. Communicating with the spirit world takes it out of one.'

'We spoke to Jack Cade, the highwayman. He has a plan. But he needs our help,' Kate hesitated, 'particularly yours . . .'

'Right. Well, go on. Spit it out.'

'What they propose is . . .'

Sylvia Craggs listened carefully as Kate repeated Jack's plan to her. Far from objecting, she positively relished the prospect. These children had taught her much about a world that she thought she knew already. The ghosts they spoke of – Jack Cade, Polly Martin, Elizabeth Hamilton, the mute boy, Govan – they were part of the city's ghostlore. The Society had files on them all. But she had never thought of them as *real*. She had regarded them as earthbound spirits, and as such they were freaks, anomalies. Interesting subjects for study and research, but with no place in this world. Now she felt differently. They meant no harm, unlike others . . .

She knew about the Judge, too. She knew the story of 'Hanging Andrews' and his Bloody Assizes, how he had sent so many to their deaths, only to meet the same fate on his own gallows. And she knew all about his house. The Society had a file a foot thick on No. 1 Fiddler's Court. She had been there often over the years. Just recently, she had gone with Eugene on his preparatory visit. He had concentrated his attention in the basement. That is where he intended to set up his equipment. She had thought at the time that the room he'd chosen seemed particularly innocent. But there was another room, the one Jack Cade called the Room of Audience. She had been in there, too, on a different visit. It was a conference room now, but even recalling it gave her a shudder. It was as cold as the grave in there. As soon as she walked in, she had sensed something malevolent, hateful, an evil influence exuding malice.

The demonstration would go on, but not, perhaps, exactly as planned. Why should Eugene Hutton have it all his own way? Her black eyes gleamed with satisfaction.

11

Friendly Fire

Tom came back just as the guests for that evening's demonstration were beginning to gather. Some had come up to the offices to speak to Mrs Craggs, while others waited down in Fiddler's Court. They were an odd bunch. Old professor-types and women of a certain age, like Mrs Craggs herself, obviously life-long members of the Society, mixed with younger people – long-haired New Age-types – and a sprinkling of what looked like journalists. Kate almost thought to see a TV crew or two. Not this time, Tom informed her. Eugene was saving that for the next demonstration, depending how this one went.

'Did you find out how it all worked?' she asked him.

'You bet,' Tom grinned. 'Me and Eugene,' he held up crossed fingers, 'we're like that.'

'So how *does* it work?' his sister asked.

'You wouldn't understand.'

'Try me.' Elinor looked at him, her eyes glinting impatience.

'First he uses infra-sound.'

'What's that?'

'See – I said you wouldn't understand . . .'

'Give me a chance!' Elinor frowned. 'Explain properly.'

'Yes, Tom,' Kate added. 'We're just as good at science as you are. We just don't show off about it. So get on with it.'

'Okay, okay,' Tom began again, speaking slowly. 'He has this machine that produces very low frequency sound waves. These force the ghosts to reveal themselves. Then he has another machine that sends out electromagnetic pulses. These zap the ghosts right out of existence. The whole process is captured on special film and video using infra-red and digital imaging.'

'How can that work?' Kate interrupted.

'I'm not sure exactly. It's a special recording system designed originally by the military for night operations.'

'I don't mean that.' Kate shook her head. 'I mean how can he zap them? Ghosts are from another dimension.'

'Oh, right. Well, electromagnetism is a very potent force. It can bring down jumbo jets. Ghosts might exist in another dimension, but they exist in the same universe. And it would work on all of them, as far as I can see. I don't see how it could discriminate between friend and foe, nice or nasty.'

'Good,' Kate said. 'We were rather counting on that.'

'What are you talking about?'

'Jack's got a plan.'

Kate left Elinor to explain what it was. Mrs Craggs was beckoning to her. It was nearly time to leave for the Judge's house.

'I like the idea,' Tom whispered as they crossed Fiddler's Court to the Judge's house. 'Friendly fire.'

'Friendly fire?' Kate had never heard the term used before. 'What's that?'

'It's like in a war when you get whacked by your own side.'

'Oh, right.'

Mrs Craggs turned, motioning them to be quiet. The group were going up the steps and filing into No. 1 Fiddler's Court.

Just as the last person went in, a smartly dressed young woman with silver-blonde hair came up the steps. She looked like a reporter, with a tape recorder over her shoulder. No one challenged her, or thought to see her invitation, as she slipped in through the closing door.

Eugene Hutton took his place several steps up on the wide staircase, ready to address the small crowd gathered in the hall in front of him.

'Any questions?' He looked round at the assembled company after he had finished speaking, rubbing his hands together in satisfaction. His speech had gone down rather well. It had also been pretty comprehensive. The group in the hall looked at each other and then back towards him. 'In that case, without more ado, I suggest we go down to the basement.'

'Just a minute,' Mrs Craggs called up from the back of the crowd. Faces turned towards her. People made way for her as she came forward. She was well known and respected. 'Might I suggest a change of venue?'

'What?' Eugene Hutton was utterly taken aback. He had not expected that. 'But why?'

'You might have the room of your choice rigged in some way.' Mrs Craggs was on the stairs now, addressing the assembled company. She turned to the man at her side, towering over him. 'I would not for a moment wish to imply that you would do such a thing, but it has been known.' She looked down at the people in front and received a few nods of agreement. 'Even if some of us are unconvinced about these mechanical methods, we all agree that

83

this is an important demonstration in the history of the Society.' She paused and got even more nods. Tom smiled. You had to admire how she was working the crowd. 'A *blind* testing, in a room of *our* choosing, would eliminate any suggestion of trickery, avoid the slightest hint of fraud, would it not, Eugene? Surely you agree?'

The people in front of them were turning to each other, muttering agreement. They seemed to decide something between them, almost without speaking. They looked back at Eugene, quiet and expectant. He let his head drop in acknowledgement, knowing that he'd lost.

'Splendid!' Mrs Craggs looked round, confident that the group was with her. 'Now which room?'

'Perhaps we should do a tour?' someone suggested.

'Don't need to,' a small grey-haired man spoke up. 'You want the conference room at the back.' He turned to the others. 'I ought to know. I was a clerk here. All the time I worked here, that room was never right.'

'It does have a reputation,' someone else agreed. 'It used to be the chambers of the old Judge himself.'

'What Judge?' her neighbour asked.

'Judge Andrews. Don't you know about him?

84

Pious as you please by day, busy hanging half the population. Different story by night. Slipping by the side door into Blythe Lane to lead a double life . . .'

'Thank you, Margery,' Sylvia said. Margery Simpson was a fund of local lore and knowledge. She was also a fellow psychic. She had alerted them to the activity at the Tourist Information Office, where she worked as a cleaner. 'Any other suggestions?' Sylvia Craggs looked around. People shook their heads, impatient now for the demonstration to begin. 'Very well. The conference room it is.'

'I'll help you with that, shall I?' Tom stepped forward to give Eugene Hutton a hand with his aluminium box.

'There's really no need . . .'

The man was getting flustered now, sweating. Tom smiled at him.

'It's no problem.'

The conference room was high-ceilinged and long, with a large fireplace of black-veined marble at one end. The walls were covered in wood panelling and rows of tall bookshelves holding volumes of legal histories and case studies. Eugene Hutton directed Tom to put the box down on the long central table. Several people shivered as they entered. This was evidently a 'cold spot'. There was a general feeling among the psychics present that the clerk had made a good choice when he'd suggested this room.

No one sat down. They ranged themselves behind the chairs drawn up to the table, or stood with their backs against the walls.

'I'm not sure that this is going to work . . .' Eugene said as he unpacked his equipment.

'I'm sure it is,' Mrs Craggs remarked with conviction. 'Many of us already feel the presences.' Her fellow psychics nodded confirmation. 'If you want us to believe in what you are doing, Eugene, you had better get on with it.'

Downstairs in the basement, the room that Eugene Hutton had actually earmarked for his experiment was packed to the rafters with ghosts. There were so many in there now that the Sentinels were having trouble keeping order, which was all part of Jack's plan. Polly was here, Govan with her. Elizabeth joined them, going to help the sick and wounded. Davey stayed by Jack, although he wasn't feeling too well himself. The attack had left him weak.

Davey kept an eye on the Sentinels set around the room to guard them. The cadaverous black-robed guards were normally as remote and ruthless as Darth Vader, but now they seemed agitated, upset. Maybe they did not like having to deal with these numbers, or perhaps they had their own problems. Every now and again one or the other of them would look to where the stairs led to the floor above . . .

Of course! Davey thought. They are waiting, just like us. They know. If they get caught, they go, too. He leaned back against the rough stone wall wondering what was happening on the floor above him, and closed his eyes for a moment, concentrating on Mrs C and the others, trying to sense where they might be. Sometimes it worked to try to visualise the scene . . .

Davey opened his eyes. The plan was working. The ghost-hunting party was already in the house, but they were not coming down here. They were being led away to the Judge's Room of Audience. Davey smiled for what felt like the first time in days, and went to tell Jack.

Jack's sombre expression lifted at the news.

'We'll be rid of the Judge, the Prior, the whole crew of them!' He grinned down at Davey. 'We will defeat them yet!'

'Save your breath, highwayman,' a voice sneered above him. '*You* will not be defeating anyone.'

Davey looked up to see Prior Robert. Extremely tall and thin, black robes draped from his skeletal limbs, he towered over them. His eyes gleamed malice from deep inside their fleshless sockets. A lipless grin stretched and creased his death's head face, taking the parchment skin close to cracking. The Prior was chief and most terrifying of all the spectral Sentinels. Davey had never seen him this close before. He flinched back, moving to Jack for protection.

'Do not look to him for help. His days are counted and there will be no returning.' He inclined his hooded head towards Jack. 'The Judge is closing the Book on you and all the rest here.'

He referred to the Book of Possibilities. Within it was recorded: *What Was, What Is, And What Is To Be*. To have the Book closed on you meant to have your name removed. Jack's jaw tightened. That meant you no longer existed.

'The Judge cannot do that,' he replied. 'He does not have the authority.'

'Who is to stop him?' The Prior laughed, a thin rusty creak of a sound. 'Look around, highwayman. The Judge can do as he likes. You have lost. He has won. I cannot tarry in idle chatter. He wishes to see one of you for an audience.'

The presence of the Prior had reduced the ghosts to hushed silence. The dread word, 'audience,' was greeted with sighs of horror and sharp intakes of breath. Jack stood up, brushing the straw from his breeches.

'Not you.' The Prior pointed a bony finger at Davey. 'He wants this boy here.'

12

The Cleansing

'Many hands make light work, Eugene,' Mrs Craggs said, and clapped her hands.

She had felt Davey's presence like a fleeting visitation. With him came the impression that the sooner this was over, the better for all, both living and spirit. She herself did not understand the assembled technology: different kinds of cameras, and the matt black boxes with their various dials, LED counters and digital display screens. There were others present who did, however, including Tom and a young man from one of the paranormal magazines. Since Eugene no longer seemed keen to continue with his experiment, she directed these others to set it up instead.

'Is everything ready?'

The people stationed at various points round the room nodded.

'Wait, wait!' Eugene Hutton stepped forward.

'For what, Eugene?' Mrs Craggs asked coldly. 'Either this works or it doesn't. We are here to find out. If it does, you will be famous. If it doesn't—'

'It's not that!' Eugene's hands twisted in agitation. 'I need to be in touch with my spirit guide . . .'

Eugene had been frantic to contact Prior Robert, to make sure that he knew about the change of venue. He could sense him in the building somewhere, and coming nearer . . . He only needed to delay for a little longer . . .

'I don't think so, Eugene. Besides, your spirit guide could be damaged,' Mrs Craggs nodded to the machinery. 'You said so yourself.'

'I know but—'

'You told me that this technology supersedes spirit guides,' Mrs Craggs smiled, 'renders such contact obsolete.'

'Yeah,' a young man with a ponytail agreed. 'You wrote an article about that for *GhostWorld*.'

Mrs Craggs smile widened. 'So why do you need yours here now?'

'Well, I, I . . .' Eugene blustered.

'We've wasted enough time,' Mrs Craggs' voice was suddenly brisk and efficient.

'You *can't* proceed—'

'Why not? We don't need your permission.'

'It's my machinery.' Eugene Hutton reached out for the button.

'It's not *yours*, Eugene. The Society funded you.'
She looked round the assembly. 'I call upon any
members here present . . .'

A forest of hands voted for the experiment to
proceed. No one voted against.

'Unanimous. Now, are you ready?' Mrs Craggs
looked round, again receiving nods in the affirmative
from those stationed at various points in the room.
'Very well.' Hands moved, fingers hovering over
various switches and buttons. 'On a count of three.
One, two . . .'

The Judge stood in front of his wide table, a white-
wigged, black-gowned figure. His fingers rested on
the Book of Possibilities closed in front of him; long
twisted claw-like fingernails scoring the calfskin
binding. His war with the other ghosts, led by Jack
and his crew, was finished. The Book was closed
upon them. Soon they would no longer exist.
Thanks to Prior Robert and the living ghost-hunter.
At the last moment, the Judge had sent the Prior to
get the boy, Davey. He did not want him caught up
in the general destruction. He might have other
uses . . .

The Judge paused, interrupting his own line of
thought. He looked round his great Room of Audience, his thin nostrils flaring. Something was amiss.

He looked towards his assembled Sentinels. They sensed it too and were stirring uneasily. He wished the Prior would return to interpret the changes going on around him. Despite the Judge's great power, he lacked the ability to move between one world and another, but he was sensitive, as all ghosts were, to certain kinds of presence.

He pulled his gown closer, beginning to shiver. The sense of intrusion was getting stronger. A strange deep noise started up. The Judge thought it must be from the cellar, marking the beginning of the Cleansing; but then the candles around him guttered, plunging the room into darkness. The booming sound grew louder. Across the room, his Sentinels sank to their knees, ears covered, mouths contorted in silent screams. A blue-green light sprang up, faint at first but getting stronger, a circle of unearthly fire, eating into the edges of the blackness. The light played across the table, crackling over the Book Of Possibilities, moving over the Judge's robes, outlining his form. The Judge stood transfixed, unable to move, his black eyes reflecting the strange flickering flames. For the first time in his life, he experienced fear.

Seconds before the demonstration began, the young woman journalist slipped out from the back of the crowd. Few people noticed as she glided out through the door. They were too intent on watching the room in front of them, wondering what was going to happen . . .

The Prior pushed Davey up the stone steps from the basement and through the stout wooden door that led in to the main part of the house where the ghost-hunting party was already assembled. Davey deliberately walked slowly, trying to play for time. Once he entered that room, he would be blown away, along with the Judge and everyone else. The Prior gave a guttural growl of impatience and prodded bony fingers into Davey's shoulder, forcing him on.

Davey wondered if he should tell him what he knew. After all, the Prior would be destroyed, too. It was worth a chance. Even if the Prior did not believe him, even if he thought that Davey was out to deceive him, any delay would be to Davey's advantage.

At the top of the steps, they turned into a stone-flagged ground floor passage made narrow by a number of iron-bound chests and heavy pieces of furniture set against dark wood panelling. Candles flickering inside horn lanterns gave a subdued and gloomy light. Two tall white candles stood either side of a massive oak door, which Davey knew opened into the Room of Audience. He had been here before with Elizabeth and Polly Martin. He glanced to the side. Another passageway led past the stairs to the hall. Beyond that lay the front door. Davey almost made a dash for it, but the Prior's pointed fingers gripped him tightly. The door would be locked and probably guarded. There seemed to be no possibility of escape . . .

'Wait, Prior, wait.' Davey stopped and forced himself to look up into the Prior's ghastly face.

'What is it, boy?' The Prior's voice was gratingly harsh and had a sighing, unearthly quality. It was nearly as horrible as his appearance.

'There's something going on in there.' Davey nodded towards the closed wooden door. He found himself gulping for air, fear made him breathless. 'The – the,' he searched for the word the ghosts used, 'Cleansing – they switched the venue, the place where it's set to happen. The ghost-hunters are in there now. The instruments are all set up, set to go off any minute!' Davey was really beginning to panic. 'Don't you see? If we go in – they'll get us, too.'

'Yes, I see.' The Prior stood for a moment in silent thought. 'That is all to the good. The ghosts held captive there,' he pointed to the basement door, 'will become my slaves. I can be rid of the Judge and rule in his stead. But you—' he looked down at Davey, shaking him like a puppy, 'you—.' The flesh curled back from his lipless mouth. 'The Living have no place here. You have meddled enough in the life of the city. I have no intention of joining them, but you—'

Prior Robert tightened his hold on Davey, half-dragging, half-carrying him. Davey felt like a kitten about to be drowned. Prior Robert's intentions were clear. He held one hand out ready to wrench open the huge oak door. He was going to throw Davey in and then block any exit by pulling across one of the heavy wooden chests set back against the wall.

He was almost within grabbing distance of the door when a young woman came drifting out of the shadows.

'Prior?'

She held up her hand to stop him, and her voice as she addressed him had a cool, quiet, shimmering quality. She wore modern clothing, a short-skirted suit, and had a bag over her shoulder, but Davey knew her, so did the Prior. They both recoiled from eyes that glinted silver and green, like frost on the first spring leaves. It was The Lady. The Old Grey Man's daughter could change her shape. Appear in any form she liked . . .

'What do you want, Lady?' Prior Robert was almost as astonished to see her as Davey

She smiled, stepping out of the shadows. 'I care nothing for your petty power struggles with the Judge, or this squabbling between the Dead and the Living. But you cannot have this boy. He is mine. I have a claim on him. Hand him over to me.' She held out her hand with the long silver nails.

'Perhaps I do not choose to.'

'Maybe I can help you change your mind.' Her shark-like smile widened as she looked up at him with tilted narrow eyes. 'I can see to it that you rule here instead of the Judge. Or—'

'Or what?'

'I can make things very difficult. It is up to you to choose.'

The Prior stared. She was the only being Davey knew who would not shrink under his sickly phosphorescent gaze. Their eyes locked in a battle of wills. Davey was a helpless bargaining counter, caught like a pawn between them. She would not let the Prior have what she claimed as hers, but he was not about to give up his prize. Certainly not now that it had increased in value.

'I tire of this . . .'

The Lady was not known for her patience. She leaned forward, lifting the heavy iron latch, letting the big oak door swing open, just a little, so the Prior could see the fate that room held. There was the terrible low booming sound Davey recognised from before. A flicker of sickly blue-green light rippled down the edges of the door. The Cleansing had begun.

The Lady was unaffected. She was not a ghost, after all. She pushed the door open wider.

'You have made your choice, Prior.'

She stood back with a slight smile, watching the Prior warp and morph as infra-sound and electro-magnetism combined to rearrange his being. He let out a deep-throated cry, somewhere between agony and despair. His grip slackened, his hand fell away from Davey's shoulder.

Davey was feeling the effects, too. The sound was reaching down inside, numbing his mind. Every-thing was slowing down, it was like melting from the inside . . .

'Come, Davey,' The Lady held out her long silver-tipped hands to claim him. 'Only I can save you now . . .'

Davey backed away, wanting to escape both her and the door with its crackling blue light. He bumped into something that felt like billowing curtains. He fought frantically as flapping arms wrapped themselves round him like a shroud. The Prior was collapsing, falling in on himself like an empty suit of clothes. Davey struggled to escape from an enveloping blackness that smelt of earth and graveyard mould. Just when he thought that he would suffocate, he managed to heave him off. He pushed the whole scarecrow mess in the direction of The Lady. The Prior's ragged remnants fell all over her like a toppling marionette.

Davey fled, using what was left of his strength to run up the passage to the front door. There was no one there guarding it. He wrestled with the handle and let himself out, shutting the door behind him with a bang. The more barriers he put between him and that room, the more his strength came back. He paused for just a second before plunging down the steps. He didn't care where he went. He just had to get away. He took to his heels and ran out into the darkening city.

The Lady disentangled herself, stepping over what remained of the Prior with distaste. She made no move to follow Davey. She could have caught him if she had wanted to, but what sport was there in that? He would be hers soon enough. She smiled her silvery frostlit smile. She would not be three times denied, but there were more ways to the wood than one.

13

The Fiddler's Court Event

The party gathered in the conference room watched in astounded silence as the event that they had been brought here to witness unfolded around them. Eugene Hutton's system actually worked! Kate was as stunned as all the rest. The infra-sound revealed another world, in a different dimension, for all to see, not just those with the *sight*. It was like being inside a horror film. As soon as the sound waves were activated, everyone in the room experienced a moment of deep disturbance, supreme discomfort. Cold sweats, hairs creeping up the back of the neck, an awareness of some other presence, the feeling of being watched. Then, just for a second, the apparitions formed. The Judge was there in the room with them, flanked by his Sentinels. All absolutely solid, real, three-dimensional.

Across the room, Tom's fingers worked on reflex, pressing the switch to send out the electromagnetic pulses. No one living felt anything, but they all saw the apparitions begin to warp and contort, convulsing in pain and terror. Then the ghastly vision began to fade, slowly at first, then more quickly, until there was nothing. Tom stared at the place where the Judge had been standing. He would never forget those cold black eyes, staring back at him, hollow with horror, at the final moment of understanding when the Judge met his nemesis.

Then it was all over. The witnesses began to file out, discussing what they had seen in the hushed tones of those who knew themselves to have taken part in something special. The event would become a legend among those interested in paranormal phenomena; but it would not be without controversy. Arguments were breaking out already. Nobody could agree that they had all seen exactly the same thing. Even the video footage and the film exposed would not convince some people. Debate was set to rage. Some swore that they saw a room in another time, a different dimension. The Judge, white wig and all, standing before a table, his hand on a great book, the robed and cowled figures of monks standing around him. Others said that they saw nothing like that, merely dark shapes and formless figures that could have been anything. Despite this, everyone agreed that something had occurred. Hutton's apparatus certainly worked. His reputation was assured. The series of stills and the footage he had on film was already worth a fortune.

He was surrounded now by a small admiring group mostly from the younger crowd. Mrs Craggs nodded at one or two and ushered the children past them.

'What about Davey?' Kate whispered when they got to the hallway.

Mrs Craggs said nothing, but led them out into the quiet little square. At the centre was a fenced-off part for residents only. A tiny patch of grass, a scattering of benches and a small play area showed through a group of trees. Rowans and silver birches, their slim trunks gleamed grey and white in the shadowy darkness. Mrs Craggs groped in her bag for a bunch of keys and, finding the right one, felt for the lock on the wrought-iron gate, turning the key to let them in. She went to the nearest seat and sat down, immediately closing her eyes. She looked old and tired, as if the whole experience was proving a little too much. The children stood in front of her, ranged round in a semi-circle. They exchanged glances. Perhaps she had gone to sleep. Perhaps . . .

Her mouth opened and closed like a fish, Kate stepped forward, convinced this time that there was something seriously wrong. Just at that moment, the woman began to speak, but not with her own voice. Elizabeth was speaking through her. The ghost girl's voice was in stark contrast to Mrs Cragg's old worn face. It was vibrant, full of joy and excitement.

'They are gone! All gone! The Judge and all his crew. What a trouncing you gave them! It is like a miracle . . .' Her tone changed to awe. 'We cannot quite believe it. We are free! The city is ours! I must go. There is much to do. All I can say now is thank you.'

'Elizabeth!' Kate spoke. 'Wait!'

'What is it?'

'Where is Davey?'

'Is he not with you?' The ghost girl sounded puzzled. 'When he did not come back and the great change came about, we assumed—' There was a catch in her voice. 'You don't mean . . . surely he wasn't caught up in the Cleansing along with the Judge and his cohorts?' Her tone turned to anguish as she realised what could have happened.

'No,' Kate said, quick to reassure her. 'We don't think that. He wasn't in the room when it happened. It's just . . . well, he's not here . . .'

'Oh.' All the jubilation left Elizabeth's voice. 'I see. Well, I'm afraid that he's not here, either.'

Davey did not even look to see the direction in which he was heading. He just ran on and on, letting his feet take him where they would. Eventually he had to stop to get his breath. He leaned against a wall, still not really taking any notice of his surroundings, only gradually becoming aware of the bulk of the cathedral towering above him. He looked up now, recognising the narrow winding street as Knowlegate, the lane that ran down by the side of the cathedral. He traced along the wall, fingers running over its rough brick surface, until he found a door. His heart skipped a beat as he recognised the low weathered stone arch and the grey pillar supports, all worn and wasted, eroding away to sand. The latch in the door felt as thin as paper, half-eaten through by rust. With trembling fingers he moved it up and pushed on silvered wood, polished smooth by the pressure of many palms. The door swung open, letting him into the garden.

He stepped on to the brick path and pale moths fluttered up all around, rising from petals glimmering white in the gathering darkness. The door closed behind him and Davey stood quiet, breathing in the heady complex scent of many herbs and flowers.

He looked round warily and then relaxed. He was back in his own time. Crisp packets and plastic sandwich boxes stuck out of the top of a litter bin. A small metal notice warned: 'Keep Off the Grass'. Something told him that he would be safe here. He walked to a nearby bench and sat down. His legs felt wobbly all of a sudden. So much had happened, first with the ghosts, then The Lady . . . He was so tired. He didn't want to think about it now.

It wouldn't hurt to rest, just for five minutes. He lodged his elbow into the corner of the curved iron arm and, using his hand as a pillow, he closed his eyes, never doubting that he would be safe from enemies, whether they were ghosts or fairies. Nothing could harm him here.

He woke suddenly, with no idea where he was, only knowing that someone was shaking him. Davey looked up and his alarm turned to terror. A tall figure dressed all in black was towering over him. He thought for a second that it was Prior Robert, escaped and come after him, pursuing him even into his own time. He tried to squirm out from under the gripping hand, backing away, flattening himself against the bench.

'It's all right. It's all right . . .'

The voice was deep and calming. The hand on his shoulder was large but gentle. Davey took a deep breath and felt his heartbeat settle. He was not looking at a spectre. This was a man. He was tall and was wearing long black clerical robes, but the hand on Davey's shoulder was warm and the eyes gazing down were blue and kind.

'I didn't mean to alarm you,' the man was saying, 'I just wondered what you were doing here. It's late and the cathedral is closed.' He pushed a hand through his thick shock of white hair and looked at Davey for a moment. When he spoke again, his voice was even quieter, his tone filled with compassion. 'Have you nowhere to go?'

'Oh, no.' Davey sat up, catching his drift. The man must think he was homeless. 'I mean, yes. My name is Davey – Davey Williams. I live in Wesson. Wesson Heath.' He found himself parroting his name and address as if he was five. 'I – er – just,' he looked around at the quiet garden swamped in shadow, 'I must have just fallen asleep.'

'Oh, I see. Good thing I happened along, then. You could have been here all night.' He held out his hand to help Davey up. 'My name's Michael, Michael Campion. Pleased to meet you Davey. I'm Provost here.'

They walked round the garden to the gate opposite. Normally this was locked but the Provost had the key for it.

'There has been a garden here for many centuries,' he said. 'I like to think it goes back to St Wulfric. The monks planted herbs for their medicines and for

106

the kitchen, but also for the beauty and scent they gave and the insects they attract. I often slip in here on a still night like this. I find it a good place to think. Now,' he looked down at Davey, 'we'd better see about telling your mum where you are and getting you home.'

Alison Williams, Davey's mother, was not too impressed about making two trips into the city, first to get Davey, then to collect Kate and his cousins. She accepted that it was a genuine mix-up, but they were still very late and she had been worried. As the eldest, and therefore the most responsible, Kate caught the worst of it. But it was her birthday the next day, and there was no point in going on too much and spoiling the occasion for everyone. Not now that they were all back safe and sound.

14

Mayday Fair

Every year, on May Bank Holiday, the fair came to town. It had done so, around about this time, for centuries. It was a genuine funfair, with rides and sideshows, set up in the very heart of the city, the streets cordoned off all around. Because it was near her birthday, when she was small, Kate had thought that it was there in honour of her. She now knew better, but she had adopted it anyway as an unofficial extension of her own celebrations. The twins usually stayed over to join in with Kate and Davey and their friends. They would all go into the city together in one great big gang.

This had once been a horse fair, a trading fair, and still attracted people from everywhere. Itinerants of every kind: gypsies, tinkers, hippies, New Age travellers, traders, conmen, tricksters, musicians. The Blind Fiddler had come as a young man with his violin under his arm, and bright blue eyes like chips of turquoise, and had never gone away. The Great Fair, as it was known in those days, attracted others. Mayday, the old Celtic festival of Beltane, is one of the hinges of the year. One of the special times when the fabric between the different worlds grows thin. The fair began in the hours of twilight and went on until midnight. Twilight is one of the hinges of the day.

The streets were crowded and not just with the Living. This was one of the nights when ghosts could join the jostling crowd and this year they were there in force. They had something to celebrate, after all. They were finally free from the Judge's tyranny. In honour of this they were holding their own great gathering and it mattered little to them that the gathering place was right in the middle of the fairground.

The more acceptable-looking ghosts went on rides and had a go on the coconut shies, just like their human counterparts. Those too ghastly to pass had their fun somewhere else. They took their places in the Ghost Train and Haunted House. Genuine ghouls lurked in among the plastic skeletons and painted spooks, shrieking and swooping as the train rattled past. Customers came out of the swinging doors, wide-eyed with wonder or shaking with terror. Sideshow holders scratched their heads as they received complaints and compliments about things that just shouldn't be there.

The ghosts fitted in so well, that even Kate failed to notice them, until a hand tapped her on the shoulder and a voice in her ear said, 'Good evening, Mistress Kate.'

Kate turned to find Jack Cade standing by her side. The highwayman did not look out of place. In white shirt and black breeches, dark hair tied back with a ribbon, and a scarf looped loosely round his neck, he looked as though he could be selling jewellery on one of the hippie stalls.

His dark eyes sparkled as he asked her, 'How do you enjoy the fair?'

'Great,' she smiled up at him. 'I love it. We come every year.'

'So do we.' He returned her smile.

'I've never seen you.'

His grin widened. 'That is because you've not been looking.'

'Where are the others?'

Kate gazed round her and suddenly she saw Govan and Elizabeth smiling at her and Polly browsing on a nearby stall.

'There are many of us here,' Jack smiled. 'It is our last great gathering. We are leaving the city.'

'When?' Kate was shocked to hear that.

'Soon. Midsummer's Eve. Now the Judge's power is broken, we are free to go. You must come to the city then, so we can say farewell.'

'Oh . . .'

Jack looked down at her. 'Don't sound so sad and disappointed. Our time has come. You should be glad—'

'I am, of course, it's just—' To Kate's surprise, she felt tears welling up inside her. 'I'll miss you. All of you. You've been our friends—'

'Hold, Mistress Kate,' Jack Cade laughed and shook out a snowy-white handkerchief. 'We have not gone yet.' He looked around as Kate blew her nose. 'Where is Davey? Is he not with you?'

Kate turned, surprised. He'd been right by her, not a minute ago.

'He must have gone off by himself somewhere,' she said.

'Oh,' Jack frowned. 'I was thinking to warn him . . .'

'About what?'

'There are folk of all sorts here, not just ghost and Living—'

'I don't follow . . .'

Kate's shake of the head forced the highwayman to be more explicit, although he was loathe to speak of them, especially here and at a time such as this.

'I mean the Host.' He dropped his voice and drew nearer, as though not wishing to be overheard. 'I speak of The Lady—'

'She's here?' Kate looked round in alarm. 'Right now?'

Jack nodded. 'And not alone. She will have others with her. The fair folk love a fair.'

'What does she want with Davey? I thought that she'd forgotten—'

Jack gave a hollow laugh. 'Her kind never forgets. They bear grudges for centuries.'

'What will she do to him?'

'I don't know,' Jack shrugged. 'But she does not wish him well, you can depend on that. I will alert the other ghosts and we will look out for him as best we can. Meanwhile my best advice is to find him and get him away before they can do him harm.'

'I certainly will,' Kate frowned. 'Thanks, Jack.'

'Think nothing of it. All the ghosts have a special care for Davey. He is quite a hero, you know.'

'Was that Jack?' Tom asked when Kate got back to her cousins standing by the dodgems.

'Yes. Have you seen Davey?'

Tom shook his head. 'But we just met Elizabeth, didn't we, El?'

'She said The Lady was about and to look out for Davey.' Elinor shivered. She had seen The Lady only once, at Hallowe'en, but once was enough. Just thinking about her was enough to bring on a panic attack. 'We have to find him, and fast.'

She looked round, eyes searching the crowds. Next to Davey she was the most sensitive. The other two regarded her with alarm.

'What do you mean, El?' Kate asked.

'I'm not sure.' She hugged herself and shivered again, even though the night was warm. 'I just have a feeling, that's all.'

Normally Elinor's 'feelings' sent her brother off into a fit of scoffing. Not this time.

'What's it telling you, Ellie?' he asked her gently.

'That if we don't hurry, we'll be too late.'

Elinor looked up at her brother, the expression in her eyes turning to fear.

'Okay,' Tom turned to Kate. 'Where did you last see him?'

Kate indicated over by the waltzers.

'We'll start there and comb right through the fair. One end to the other. Sticking together. All right?'

They set off, arms linked, Tom looking straight ahead, Kate to the left, Elinor to the right. They scoured the stalls and the arcades, the sideshows and different attractions scattered through the streets all around. But their searching was concentrated on the ground; it did not occur to any of them to look up for quite some time . . .

Davey loved fairs and this was his favourite. Although the rides were fewer and small in comparison, for him it beat theme parks or seaside fairgrounds. He loved the hot smell of candy floss and diesel and he loved the way the streets were taken over. All normal life was swept aside in the rush and swirl of the rides, the bright garlands of garish lights and the brash echoing boom of music hugely amplified.

He'd lost the others ages ago. He liked to savour the fair alone, to go round on his own, sampling this and that. The day had been warm and bright, and was just fading into night. He stood breathing in the atmosphere, the rich mix of conflicting smells. To the diesel oil and candy floss, he added onions, burgers and hot dogs. Above him, riders shrieked and whooped, swooping through the gathering darkness, calling like high strange birds as their carriages twisted and turned through snaking necklaces of light. It was like stepping into magic.

He longed to go up on the rollercoaster, but the fare was dear, and he didn't have any money left. He felt in his pockets. His sampling had taken quite a toll on his finances. He was all spent up. He was just about to troop off miserably when he notice[d] [some]thing down on the ground. A tightly folde[d] [piece of] paper glinting orange and bronze in the gu[tter? He] bent down, thinking it was a discarded ticke[t from] one of the stalls, but his fingers unfolded a ten pou[nd] note. Davey looked around furtively, thinking he should hand it in to somebody, but knowing he had no intention of doing so. He folded it back into the palm of his left hand, ready to give it to the man who ran the ride.

Someone opened the door. Someone else flipped up the bar and Davey got down from the car. His legs were shaking. He came out past the pay booth to find Tom waiting for him. Tom had finally sussed that he could be on the ride and had been there to meet every car. Tom frowned as Davey came towards him down the ramp. He was holding on to the rail like a little old man.

'Wow!' Tom commented. 'That must have been some ride!'

His cousin's face was pale, the freckles stood out like dots sprayed across it. His eyes, wide and black, seemed all pupil. He looked like he was about to throw up.

'Yeah,' Davey replied in a whisper. 'Yeah, it was.'

'How long have you been on it?'

avey did not reply, just shrugged.

'You the only one to get off?' Tom looked past his cousin. No one else was with him.

'Yeah. The others must've paid to go again.'

Tom looked up. The car crawling up the steep incline to the start of the ride was empty.

'Are you sure, Davey, mate?' He nodded his head towards the rollercoaster track. 'It looks like there's no one in it to me.'

'Sure?' Davey turned slowly, his eyes still dilated and unfocused. 'Of course I'm sure . . .'

Davey would never forget that ride, or those who had ridden with him. They had enjoyed it as much as he had. Their slanting eyes had glittered, igniting with excitement as the car plunged and twisted round the track. Their high wild cries seemed to make it go faster, as if they could make it take off. They rode standing, arms out as if they were flying, their hair streaming behind them like wind-blown fire.

'Are you all right?' Tom asked, his sandy brows drawn together in a puckered frown.

'Yeah. 'Course,' Davey looked back at him. 'Why shouldn't I be?'

'No reason,' Tom shrugged. 'Let's find Kate and El.'

'Okay.'

Davey followed Tom obediently enough, but Tom thought his cousin was acting strangely, even for Davey.

Kate thought so, too. She phoned her dad to come and get them. They had all had enough of the fair by then. Their father arranged to meet them over the bridge in the New Town. Davey didn't object. He followed his sister and cousins meekly, but every now and then he would turn to sneak a look at the snaking, twisting rollercoaster lights and to listen out for the shrieks and cries from the ride. He had never been so excited in his whole life as he had been up there in the sky. He had never seen people like the ones who had ridden with him, with their long flowing hair and slender limbs and shiny clothes of silver, gold and green.

Maybe they were in a rock band or something, Davey thought to himself. That must be it. There was to be a concert later on, with laser lights and everything. Kate had nagged and nagged at Mum and Dad to be allowed to go, but they had said 'no', she was still too young. Davey had not been both- ered, until now. He just wanted to see those people again. Be with them. His heart ached with a longing he had never known before. Everything around him meant nothing. They had been so glamorous. That was the word for them, he decided. Glamorous.

Glamour is an old, old word meaning to bewitch or enchant, but Davey did not know that. Neither did he realise that a glamour had been cast over him. He had stepped from the earth into the air and met the creatures who dwelt there; now he was caught in their deep enchantment, fluttering like a moth inside a lantern.

to be continued . . .

H.A.U.N.T.S

By Celia Rees

Books 1: H is for Haunting

Day and night, all through the city, ghosts of the past shadow the present – some are deadly, others mean no harm. Few mortals can slip into their world, but those who do must fight to stay alive . . .

It is Midsummer's Eve, just before dusk. Davey, Kate, Elinor and Tom embark on the city's Ghost Tour – an unforgettable journey back and forth in time, crossing an unknown and terrifying threshold.

Look out for more books in this series . . .

Another Hodder Children's Book

H.A.U.N.T.S

By Celia Rees

Books 2: A is for Apparition

Day and night, all through the city, ghosts of the past shadow the present – some are deadly, others mean no harm. Few mortals can slip into their world, but those who do must fight to stay alive . . .

It is Halloween night, and Davey, Kate, Elinor and Tom go trick-or-treating. But not all the ghosts and phantoms that roam the streets are harmless. Some are truly the living dead . . .

Look out for more books in this series . . .

H.A.U.N.T.S

By Celia Rees

Books 3: U is for Unbeliever

*Day and night, all through the city, ghosts of the
past shadow the present – some are deadly, others
mean no harm. Few mortals can slip into their
world, but those who do must fight to stay alive . . .*

It is just before Christmas and Davey receives a
warning from a trusted friend . . . A ghostly
enemy is out to get him. He must stay away from
the city centre or be caught forever in a deadly
time trap . . .

Look out for more books in this series . . .

H.A.U.N.T.S

All Hodder Children's books are available at your local bookshop or newsagent, or can be ordered direct from the publisher. Just tick the titles you want and fill in the form below. Prices and availability subject to change without notice.

Hodder Children's Books, Cash Sales Departmnt, Bookpoint, 39 Milton Park, Abingdon, OXON, OX14 4TD, UK. If you have a credit card you may order by telephone – (01253) 400414.

Please enclose a cheque or postal order made payable to Bookpoint Ltd to the value of the cover price and allow the following for postage and packing:
UK & BFPO – £1.00 for the first book, 50p for the second book, and 30p for each additional book ordered up to a maximum charge of £3.00.
OVERSEAS & EIRE – £2.00 for the first book, £1.00 for the second book, and 50p for each additional book.

Name ....

....

Address..

....

If you would prefer to pay by credit card, please complete:
Please debit my Visa/Access/Diner's Card/American Express (delete as applicable) card no:

Signature ....

Expiry Date...